Charlotte Turner Smith

Montalbert

a novel

Charlotte Turner Smith

Montalbert
a novel

ISBN/EAN: 9783337349547

Printed in Europe, USA, Canada, Australia, Japan

Cover: Foto ©Andreas Hilbeck / pixelio.de

More available books at **www.hansebooks.com**

MONTALBERT.

A NOVEL.

BY CHARLOTTE SMITH,

IN THREE VOLUMES.

VOL. III.

London:

PRINTED BY S. LOW, BERWICK STREET, SOHO;

FOR

E. BOOKER, NO. 56, NEW BOND STREET.

1795.

MONTALBERT.

CHAPTER XXV.

IT appears as if the fears, which had diſtreſſed Roſalie, had in ſome degree ſubſided when ſhe thus proceeded with her narrative, or rather journal:——

"*April* 11*th*, 1783.

"It is now above a fortnight ſince I have been here. Every day has appeared more melancholy than that which pre-ceded it; for every day and every hour diminiſhes my hope that Montalbert is

VOL. III.   B   engaged

engaged in feeking me......Alas! could his vigilant love be deceived, or would not Signora Belcaftro betray herfelf, had fhe been queftioned?—Ah! fool that I am! I recolleft that he could not queftion her; that he certainly could never know from her that Rofalie exifts—Alozzi too is interefted in deceiving him—perhaps we fhall never meet again.....Montalbert! perhaps I am doomed to pafs here, in this dreadful folitude, a long and wretched life. It is now four days fince I prevailed on Cattina to let me wander over the de-ferted grounds that were once a garden; fhe finds I make no attempt to abufe this indulgence, and fhe does not now inter-dift the woods that furround the enclo-fure, or even the fea fhore, though it is there only that I am likely to meet any of the few human beings who inhabit this depopulated region. I have been down to the fands, and on the wave-worn re-mains of a marble column, once, perhaps, the ornament of the port; I have been fitting to look at the fea. A very few

days

days since I should not have ventured hither, for then my imagination was filled with the fears that Cattina had so recently taught me, of Corsairs and Turks. By habit, and from having assured myself, by subsequent conversations, that Cattina had exaggerated and misdated her accounts, I had appeased those apprehensions, or learned to think of them with more steadiness: nor, indeed, could my walks increase, whatever real danger there might be, since, during the day time, any vessel would be discerned from the coast long before it could land its crew. I saw to-day a group of peasant girls picking up the small fish along the sand; they were gay and sportive, and seemed to have no fear of such visits as Cattina has described to me as frequently happening. I wished to have spoken to them; but, perhaps, I ought to consider it as a part of my convention with Cattina, not to enter into conversation with any of the persons I may chance to meet.—Alas! these poor

Calabrese

Calabrese could be of no use to me: they seemed to have no ideas beyond the little circle of their own necessities or pleasures; for though they must have known me to be a stranger, I excited no curiosity. Their happy indifference brought to my mind days when I was as thoughtless and as light-hearted as these simple peasants! That reflection was followed by the recollection of the circumstances that have happened to me within these last two years, and the chain of events, which, from one of the happiest, had reduced me to one of the most miserable of women. My waking dream lasted till the sun was set; the waves, as well as the whole horizon, assumed that rosy hue which mocks alike the pencil and the pen; I had heard that the exhalations from the marshes were unwholesome after a warm day, and I returned to my melancholy residence lest my child should suffer. Now, Montalbert, that he is sleeping by me, I relate on paper the sad employment of my solitary day—

day—alas! how many more may pafs in the fame manner—what a profpeſt is mine!

" It is night.—I go to my window and look at the ſtars, which, in this clear atmoſphere, are ſingularly brilliant. I feek the north ſtar, becauſe, Montalbert, I believe that you are in England—an idea that fometimes torments and fometimes fooths me; yet I encourage it even when I am moſt pained by it, for you have returned thither, perhaps, if not to feek your Roſalie, to weep with her mother for her ſuppoſed death. . . . . That dear mother!—ah! how many tears have I already coſt her—how many will ſhe ſhed over my imaginary grave; while I, buried yet living, call on her name—on yours, Montalbert, in vain!

" Perhaps it is fit we ſhould fuffer thus—perhaps it is the proper puniſhment for our difobedience. . . . . Oh! if it be fo, may I alone be purfued by the vengeance of Heaven, and may that little innocent creature be fpared and reſtored to the

B 3   proteſtion

protection of his father. It is possibly to me, to my rash folly, that Montalbert owes much of his present uneasiness: his mother may have driven him from her with reproaches, with anger—he may, on my account, be loaded with a parent's curse!——Dreadful thought! I dare not dwell upon it.

"I cast my eyes round the high and gloomy room where I sit: all is silent and forlorn; cold and faint, my heart seems to sink within me, and I listen, with even a degree of eagerness, to hear the flow footsteps of Cattina, along the apartments, bringing me my evening meal.

"My keeper, for what else can I call her, is gone; she seems every day to soften in her manners towards me, and especially since she finds my child is to be brought up in the religion of his father. Poor, prejudiced woman; but she has not a bad heart, and there is something respectable even in her prejudices. I complained to her, this evening, of the languor I felt for want of some amusement when my

child

child flept; and I afked if there were no books to be obtained here?—It was fome time before I could make her under-ftand my queftion. At length, however, fhe told me, that at the farther end of the caftle, in a room which is never opened, there are a great many papers, and fhe believes books; fhe promifes to fhew it me to-morrow. I may meet with fome Italian poets, who may beguile thofe te-dious minutes in which I am now tortured with my own thoughts. How well I re-member, at Barlton Brooks, exploring the library of Mr. Leffington, and with as little fuccefs as I fhall probably have to-morrow.

" But talking to this woman has a little relieved my fpirits; for even the found of a human voice is confoling to my ear!

" I will now endeavour to fleep.....
Oh, come! thou image of my adored Mon-talbert—not as laft night, in imaginary dan-ger and contention, and rifquing, for my defence, a life more precious than my own—but come to whifper peace and hope

to

to the dreams of your devoted Rosalie!—
Ah! would I could be assured that you
will ever read my journal; that your eye
will ever mark where the tears have blis-
tered the paper as I write this, perhaps,
fruitless wish!

                  " *April* 13*th*.

  " I look back at my journal of yester-
day, and of the preceding day, and am
half-tempted to give up this monotonous
account of lingering anguish. I have learned nothing by my research after books,
but the great extent of this my prison,
and that it is Formiscusa, a castle situated
seventeen miles from Squilace, and was
the seat of feudal government, when the
Norman Barons possessed this country.
A rude map or chart, hung up against
the walls of the room I explored yester-
day, has told me this; but not without
my taking some pains to get at the intelligence, by clearing away the mould with
which it was covered, and, like many
others, I have sought only my own pain;
                       for

for I now fee that, from the fituation of the place, there is but too much reafon to believe it muft be, at all times, expofed to hoftile vifits from Africa, or Turkey in Europe. I thought I had reafoned my-felf out of thefe fears, but they return in fpite of me—fo prone is the human mind, when under the preffure of actual evils, to aggravate them by anticipation of the future.

" You would chide me, Montalbert, for any tendency to indulge this difpofition.— Ah! wretch that I am, if you were here, fhould I murmur?—fhould I dream of evil?——Ah!—no—with you, this folitary and frowning pile would be to me a Pa-radife! I fhould then enjoy the beauty of a country, which, in fome parts, is really lovely, but over which my eyes now wander often half-blinded by tears.

" Since I have had permiffion to go out, however, and have walked about the garden, I am better; for there is a charm, in the contemplation of vegetable nature, that fooths my fpirits beyond every thing

but

but mufic..... When poor Rofalie Leffington was ill at eafe, at Barlton Brooks,
it was a feat on the turf of the downs,
under the fhade of an old thorn or a
tufted beech, that fhe retired to figh at
liberty, though fhe then hardly knew why
fhe fighed. Now the really unhappy Rofalie Montalbert, with her infant in her
arms, and, ah! with fenfations how different in her heart, finds a refting place
on the plinth of a broken ftatue, or on a
piece of granite rock, fhaded with myrtle
or embowered in arbutus, and furveys,
with hopelefs eyes, the fun finking into
the fea, from whence he will arife to-
morrow to bring to her another day of
tears and defpair!

" Juft as I had finifhed the laft fentence, Cattina came to tell me, that a
Turkifh xebec, chafed by a Maltefe galley, was in fight; and that I might now
be convinced how very near the Barba-
rians fometimes approached the fhore.
I trembled, and had hardly ftrength to
follow her up to the weftern tower, which
affords

affords the moft extenfive view: I faw two veffels, one of which purfued the other, but they were too diftant for me to dif-tinguifh with what nations they were manned. Soon afterwards, however, they were fo near that I could diftinguifh the form of the Turkifh veffel, and fee the crefcent fhe bore as an enfign ; but fight-ing did not feem to be her purpofe at that time: for, finding the Maltefe gain upon her, fhe fet up more fail, and made every effort to get away. The enemy, however, purfued, and fired upon her; we heard the report, and foon after faw the flafhes of the guns amid clouds of fmoke; the Corfair returned the fire, but ftill made off, and, I fuppofe having fome advantage as to lightnefs, foon got out of the reach of the firing. At length the xebec be-came like a doubtful fpot in the horizon, and then entirely difappeared ; while the Maltefe veffel, to my great comfort, aban-doned the chafe, yet continued cruizing along the coaft, as if to protect us againft the invader, fhould he dare to return.

B 6   " My

" My eyes are affected by gazing fo long at the dazzling expanfe of fea, and they and my heart ftill flutter with ap- prehenfion. I dread going to bed, for I fhall fancy I hear hoftile founds in the adjoining rooms, and threatening tones in an unknown language: yet I know thefe pirates are gone, and unlikely now to moleft us.

" I went down into the garden in hopes of calming my fpirits before I attempted to fleep.—Already the heats have tarnifh- ed the lively verdure of fpring, and the cicala has began to devour the leaves; while in England the trees are but juft budding, and the earlier fhrubs hardly in leaf. If I were a poet, I fhould be tempt- ed, were my heart ever for a moment at eafe, to add one to the number of thofe who have celebrated, or have attempted to celebrate, the nightingale; for here the note of that bird is infinitely more mellow and delicious than in England. I have been vainly trying to recollect fome of the moft beautiful addreffes to this fongftrefs

of

of the night, but trouble and anxiety have driven from my memory the few images that, in my circumfcribed reading, I had once collected......... Montalbert! fhall I ever again be reftored to happinefs and you ?—If ever I am, fhall I not feel myfelf fo depreffed, fo undone, by this tedious courfe of fuffering, as to have loft the few claims I had to your tendernefs.— Ah! here is another fource of pain opened—I become a felf tormenter. But, confcious that it is weak, nay, perhaps wicked, I will try to check this continual inclination to repine—I will kneel by my fleeping infant, and recommend him and Montalbert to the protection of that merciful Being, who preferved me and my child among the crafh of ruins, and the yawning gulphs that furrounded us in Sicily, and who can deliver us from this dreary prifon, and reftore us to the hufband and the father."

The little narrative of Rofalie was now interrupted.

Wearied

Wearied by the continual famenefs of
wandering about the fortrefs, where gloomy
ftrength was not allied to fafety, and where
there was no alternative between the ftag-
nation of cheerlefs folitude and the tre-
mors of fear, (for whenever fhe converfed
with Cattina thefe fears failed not to be
renewed), Rofalie, on the day following
that of which fhe has laft given an account,
took a walk hitherto untried, and went
down to the village, if a fmall group of
fifhermen's huts could be called fo.—
Thefe were built with pieces of marble,
intermingled with clay, and among them
lay fcattered many remains of magnificent
buildings, pieces of large ftatues, and
broken pillars. The idea of the fplendid
works of man fallen to decay, and haftening to oblivion, yet having furvived for
ages the beings who toiled to raife them,
has always fomething mournful in it to
a reflecting mind; and Rofalie was ima-
gining to herfelf how different the appearance of this port muft have been fe-
ven

ven hundred years ago, when it was crowded with veffels, and its ftreets difplayed all that commerce then procured for the rich and luxurious. Now, ftrange reverfe! a few half-naked children playing before the humble doors, where their fun-burnt mothers fat fpinning coarfe hemp, or a fifherman or two pufhing off their barks with the evening tide, to fifh during the night, on the fuccefs of which, their principal fubfiftence depended, were all the living beings vifible in this obfcure hamlet.

A high mound, rifing in the midft of the village, had been formed by the fallen ruins of a temple. It was now covered with grafs and low fhrubs, but through them a marble capital, or an half-buried column, here and there were vifible. On one of thefe laft Rofalie fat down to reft a few moments before fhe returned home, and was fometimes indulging the reflections infpired by the place, fometimes talking to her child in a low and fweet voice, when fhe was ftartled by the footfteps of
a perfon

a perſon on the hollow ground near her; ſhe looked ſuddenly up, and ſaw, not an Algerine pirate, but a gentleman, whom ſhe immediately knew to be an Engliſhman.

Her amazement prevented her either moving or ſpeaking; while the ſtranger, taking off his hat, ſaid—" You muſt forgive me, Madam, if I cannot repreſs my curioſity—I believe you are Engliſh?— I fear I may appear impertinent; but it is impoſſible for me to reſtrain the eager wiſh I have to know by what extraordinary circumſtance I here find a perſon ſo unlike the inhabitants—ſo unlike the objects I came hither to ſeek?"

However reſpectfully this addreſs was made, there were places and occaſions where Roſalie would have reſented it as impertinent; but now, on the deſert coaſt of Calabria, an Engliſhman ſeemed to her as a brother—and the accents of an Engliſh voice, as a voice from Heaven.

She tried, however, in vain to anſwer diſtinctly the unexpected queſtion thus
made,

made, and, faltering and trembling, faid, in a voice hardly articulate, " I do not wonder, Sir, you are furprized at feeing me here! I am, indeed, an Englifh ftranger, and brought hither by a feries of events too long to relate."—At that moment fhe recollected, that, if fhe was feen fpeaking to any one, her walks would be put an end to, and her confufion increafed. She took courage, however, to add—" I am detained here wholly againft my inclinations, and defpair ever to revifit my native country......I thank you, Sir, for the intereft you feem to take in my misfortunes; but I dread being feen to converfe with -------"

" Haften then, I conjure you, (cried the Englifhman), to tell me where you live, and how I can be of ufe to you....Good God! you are here againft your inclinations!—But who dares to confine you?—I am a ftranger to you, Madam, and a mere idle wanderer in this land; but, as a man of your country, you have

a right

a right to all my fervices—command, and
be affured I will at leaft try to obey
you."

A ray of hope now darted into the mind
of Rofalie. Prepoffeffed with an idea that
Montalbert was in England, the offers of
this gentleman feemed to be directed by
the interpofition of Heaven to convey her
to him. The tumult of her fpirits were
too great to allow her to reflect on the
hazard fhe might incur by putting herfelf
into the power of a ftranger ; the hopes of
being conveyed to England, and Montalbert, by his means, abforbed at that
moment every other confideration : but
the more delightful the profpect was, the
more fhe dreaded its vanifhing, and this
fhe knew would happen if Cattina difcovered her talking to any one.

Terrified, therefore, left fhe fhould be
obferved, fhe faid, in a hurried way—
" I am fo fituated, that I dare not ftay
to explain who I am, or relate the caufes
that have made me a prifoner in the great
castle

caftle you fee above ; but, if you are in the neighbourhood of this place to-morrow - - - - - - - -''

" If I am ? (cried the ftranger eagerly), only tell me where I fhall fee you again, and I will wait your own time—I will attend you at the rifk of my life."

" I hope, (interrupted Rofalie tremuloufly)—I hope there will be no rifk. . . . . If you will be, at five o'clock to-morrow evening, in a fmall wood, which is the boundary of a fort of garden on the other fide of the caftle, near a place where the remains of feveral ftatues furround a ruined fountain - - - - - - - ; (fhe recollected that fhe was making an affignation with a man fhe had never feen before, and ftopped, for fhe felt all the impropriety of it ; yet, encouraged by her motives and the rectitude of her intentions, fhe proceeded)——I will be there, and explain to you who I am, and how - - - - you can oblige me, (fhe was going to fay, but again checked herfelf, and only added)— but now it is impoffible for me to ftay."

The

The ftranger repeated her directions with earneftnefs, and affured her he would be there.—" And this lovely child too! (faid he, ftill following her as fhe turned to go the caftle); is this too of my country?"—" It is mine, (anfwered Rofalie mournfully); but, indeed, you muft now leave me, or your obliging offers of fervice will be fruftrated."—The gentleman bowed, and fuffered her to go, following her with his eyes till fhe reached the buildings adjoining the caftle, which concealed her from his fight. He then flowly retired, while Rofalie, breathlefs and trembling, fought her guard, and fo over-acted her part, by complaining of her folitary walks, and affecting her former languor, that a more accurate obferver than Cattina would have gueffed that fome unufual circumftance had befallen her.

Cattina had, however, no fufpicions, and Rofalie went to her room, and to her reflections on what had paffed.

She

She endeavoured to recal the perion, expreffions, and manner of the ftranger to whom fhe had fpoken, that fhe might now, in a cooler moment, afk herfelf whether he appeared to be really a gentleman, and one in whom fhe ought to repofe fo much confidence as to put herfelf under his protection.——He was a young man, apparently not more than two or three and twenty; his countenance was lefs handfome than expreffive, and there was fomething remarkable in it, which Rofalie could not define. He had the air and manners of a 'gentleman; but fhe knew that many have thofe advantages whom it would be extreme imprudence to truft. Perhaps too, notwithftanding the earneftnefs with which he offered her any fervices in his power, he might fhrink from the trouble and expence of conducting her and her child to England; for young as fhe was, and little as fhe had yet feen of the world, fhe was not now to learn that thofe who

moft

moft warmly profefs friendfhip, are often thofe who fly from the performance of any kindnefs at all inconvenient to themfelves. Thefe and other reflections half difcouraged Rofalie from the plan fhe had formed, in the firft moments of meeting, with a man who feemed to have the power of releafing her. The difpofition of Montalbert forcibly recurred to her; he might be rendered for ever fufpicious of her conduct, if fhe thus rafhly entrufted herfelf to a perfon of whom fhe could know nothing, and whofe character might be fuch as would entirely ruin hers, in the opinion of the world, when it fhould be known that fhe had been conducted by him to England.— Yet, on the other hand, in lofing the only opportunity to efcape that might ever offer, fhe condemned herfelf and her little boy to perpetual imprifonment, and became accefary to her own mifery and that of Montalbert...... Ah! who could tell that he would not, in the perfuafion

of

of her death, yield to the importunities
of his mother, and marry the Roman lady
to whom fhe had fo long wifhed to unite
him. This idea was as infupportable as
that of his death, and, compared with its
being realized, every other evil became
light, and every hazard difappeared.—
Sometimes, however, the fear of her hufband's having perifhed at Meffina obtruded itfelf; but the pains his mother
had taken to conceal her argued ftrongly
againft it. But, even if fuch a calamity
had really happened, it feemed to be the
duty of his widow to claim the rights of
his child, and how could this be done
but by having recourfe to her friends in
England: for friends, fhe believed, fhe
had, not only in her mother, who would
protect and affift, though fhe could
not own her, but in Charles Vyvian her
real, and William Leffington her adopted, brother. Towards thefe fhe thought
fhe might look for protection and kindnefs; and thefe hopes, added to her
dread, of remaining for life in the melancholy

lancholy and even dangerous folitude of
Formifcufa, determined her, if the ftranger
on their meeting ftill appeared willing to
affift her, to endeavour, by his means, to
reach England.

CHAP.

CHAP. XXVI.

So various and contradictory were the thoughts which agitated Rosalie during the night, that she found it impossible to sleep; she arose with the earliest dawn, and, though so many hours were to intervene before that of her appointment, she could not forbear going to the place she had marked to her new friend for their meeting, that she might be sure she had described it accurately. She returned, however, almost immediately to the house, for, conscious of having something to hide, she now feared Cattina might suspect her.

From the windows towards the sea she now again saw the Maltese galley, which had been some days hovering on the coast. It cast anchor near the shore, a

c   boat

boat put off from it, and landed behind a fmall promontory, which formed one fide of the port. It now occurred to Rofalie, that there was fome connection between the arrival of this veffel and that of her new acquaintance. He came then from Malta, and was in all probability returning thither. If fuch was the cafe, how could he charge himfelf with her and her child?—or, admitting he would do fo, how could fhe expofe herfelf to the hazard of traverfing the fea in a Maltefe veffel, which, fhe knew, was liable to be continually engaged by Turkifh and Algerine pirates. Thefe doubts, added to thofe fhe had before, ferved to agitate her fpirits fo much, that, when the hour of appointment came, fhe had hardly ftrength to go to the fountain in the wood, where her Englifh friend had arrived before her.

Rofalie trembled, and looked fo pale as fhe advanced towards him, that, alarmed, he faid—" I hope, Madam, nothing has happened, fince I had the honour of meeting

meeting you yefterday, to give you uneafinefs?——I hope the favour you do
me, by thus condefcending to come hither --------- ''

Rofalie, whofe heart beat fo violently
that fhe was unable to fpeak, interrupted
him by a deep figh, and a faint attempt
to articulate " No, Sir! nothing has happened——only I am fo—fo—unfortunate,
and fo uncertain what is to become of
me, that --------.'' She could not
proceed, but leaned againft a tree, and
tried to recover herfelf, while the ftranger,
who was apprehenfive fhe would faint,
led her towards a piece of broken marble,
and entreated her to fit down upon it;
fhe did fo, and, in a fhort time, affured
him fhe was better, and begged his pardon for the weaknefs fhe had betrayed.

" I own, Madam, (faid the ftranger),
that my curiofity is very ftrongly excited,
and that I am impatient to know how
I can be fervicable to you? I might claim
a fort of privilege to be admitted to your
confidence, becaufe I am of the fame na-

tion;

tion; but I rather reſt my plea on the
earneſt inclination I feel to be employed
in your ſervice: if, as I fear, you are
unhappy, and ſuffering from the tyranny
of ſome relation — — — — — — — —." The
ſtranger heſitated, as if uncertain how to
proceed on a ſubjeɛt that might be of a
very delicate nature, and, from his manner, it ſtruck Roſalie as if he thought
ſhe was confined by her huſband—an im-
preſſion which might involve her in very
diſagreeable conſequences. She, therefore, took courage to ſay—" It is true
I am a priſoner at this place, and am
moſt deſirous of being releaſed, in hopes
of being reſtored to my huſband, who
would, I am ſure, be very grateful to any
one who undertook to aſſiſt me in re-
gaining my liberty—if (added ſhe) he
ſtill lives—as I will not ſuffer myſelf to
doubt."

" Good God! (exclaimed the Engliſh
ſtranger), by what accident, for it is impoſſible it ſhould be from choice, could
a man, happy enough to be your huſband,
allow

allow himſelf to be torn from you ; and who can have authority to confine you here ?"

" My ſtory is long and extraordinary, (anſwered Roſalie) ; I can only relate now, that I was ſeparated from my huſ-band in conſequence of the earthquake which deſtroyed Meſſina, and that his mother, averſe to his marriage with a wo-man of another religion and country, has taken occaſion to divide us, as ſhe hopes, for ever, by confining me here, and probably by perſuading him that I am no more."

" He is an Italian then?" cried the ſtranger.

" Born of an Italian mother, (replied Roſalie), but his father was an Engliſh-man, and of an ancient Engliſh family."— The recollection that Montalbert might at this moment believe her dead, and even be the huſband of another, added to the fear that ſhe was perhaps doing wrong, and putting herſelf into the power of a

man

man who might take bafe advantages of her confidence, were fenfations fo uneafy, that, lofing the little fortitude fhe had col-lected, fhe burft into tears.

The gentleman appeared to be really hurt at her diftrefs; and, lowering his voice, faid—" I thank you, Madam, for the confidence you have already placed in me; perhaps I ought not to expect you to truft me farther, till I tell you who it is that you fo highly honour, and by what accident I am in a part of Italy fo feldom vifited by Englifh travellers. But fuffer me to afk, if you are now fe-cure from the malicious obfervations of this Italian woman, who exercifes over you tyranny fo unjuftifiable?"

" There are only fervants in the caftle, (replied Rofalie). My perfecutors deem-ed them fufficient for the purpofe of guard-ing me in a place fo remote, that my efcape feemed impoffible...... I believe they will not moleft me here, as I am accuftomed to walk alone of an even-ing."

" Since

" Since you permit me then, (faid the
ftranger), I will relate, in a few words,
what you have a right, Madam, to know,
before I can expect you will rely on my
aſſurances, of being ready to render you
any ſervice you may honour me with;
and yet I am ſenſible that a man is never
more aukwardly circumſtanced than when
he is obliged to ſpeak of himſelf, and,
above all, to tell who he is. It is particularly difficult for me to do this, (added
he, in a dejected tone), ſince I have not
unfrequently forgotten myſelf, or, at leaſt,
been in a diſpoſition of mind which made
me very ſincerely try at it." ——

He pauſed, but Roſalie continuing
ſilent and attentive to him, he went on—

" Perhaps, if your reſidence in England
was in the weſt, you may have heard of
the family of Walſingham—I am of that
family....... It is not neceſſary to relate
to you, Madam, the particular circumſtances of a life which has had nothing
uncommon in it, unleſs it be that I loſt,
at an early period, the perſon with whom

I hoped

I hoped to have paffed it in as much happinefs as mutual affeɛtion and a coincidence of difpofition could promife.— From that time, the death of my elder brother having made the purfuit of the profeffion to which I was brought up unneceffary, I have wandered over the world, with the hope of finding, in change of place, a temporary relief for the wounds which no time can cure ; and I have fucceeded fo far, as to take fome intereft in the objeɛts which nature, or art, prefent to the traveller, particularly in Italy : as I had before vifited almoft every part of it, except Malta and Calabria ultra, and found that my fpirits once more required change of place, I left England about two months fince for Leghorn, from thence I got a paffage to Malta, and having a curiofity to vifit that part of Calabria immediately oppofite the coaft of Sicily, which had been fo lately the fcene of one of the moft tremendous convulfions of Nature on record, I embarked in a Maltefe galley, commanded by the

Chevalier

Chevalier de Montagny, a French Knigh of Malta, with whom I had been fortunate enough to make an acquaintance; and we defigned to have extended our cruize to the Gulph of Manfredonia, but having feen an Algerine or Turkifh xebec, which the Chevalier had reafon to believe was hovering about the coaft with piratical intentions, he determined to attempt taking it. We were in chafe for many hours; after which, the Chevalier cafting anchor about a mile from hence, I inquired, as I ufually do, what there was worth landing to fee?—and with fome difficulty difcovered, that we were near the ancient port of Formifcufa, where there were a few fine remnants of Roman buildings, and where I might very probably find coins, or fmall pieces of fculpture. My friend de Montagny, whofe intention it was to watch the xebec, which, he believed, intended to return, affured me, that I might come on fhore and fatisfy my curiofity without any danger of his leaving me behind. I avail-

ed

ed myfelf, therefore, of the occafion, and
had been purchafing fome antiquities, of
little value to them, among the peafants
of the village, when, furveying that fpot
where there are evidently the ruins of
a temple, I was furprifed to obferve a
lady, whom I immediately faw was very
unlike the inhabitants of the furrounding
country, and who, on my nearer approach, I heard fpeak in accents which
confirmed my firft idea of her being an
Englifhwoman.......Ah! Madam, how
happy fhall I efteem myfelf, if, in the
accidental indulgence of that curiofity,
where the higheft gratification it can afford, is but a very tranfient relief to a
mind incurably hurt, I fhould prove the
means of being effentially ufeful to a
young lady—who—I am ill at expreffing
what I feel, and know that you are, that
you muft be, fuperior to common-place
compliments: yet I cannot refrain from
faying, that, as being of the fame country, you have on that fcore a right to my
beft fervices, though, that were you of
any

any other, one need only behold you to be convinced that you muſt command the moſt reſpeſtful homage of every man."

Roſalie, who had rather the latter part of this ſpeech had been ſpared, now heſitated, bluſhed, and attempted to ſpeak, but ſhe failed; and Walſingham, who ſaw her embarraſſment, and appeared perfeſtly to underſtand it, reſumed his diſcourſe..

" Unleſs I know more of your ſituation, than, on ſo ſhort an acquaintance, you may think it proper to entruſt me with, I cannot venture to adviſe; but I can, with great truth, aſſure you, that if you will venture to put yourſelf under my care, I ſhall think it the moſt fortunate circumſtance of my life, to be allowed to conduſt you from hence, in whatever manner you think conſiſtent with ſafety or propriety, and to whatever place you ſhall point out. I will not leave you till you are ſecure in the proteſtion of ſome of your friends, and I will attend

you

you either to any part of the continent, or
to England."

Rofalie, now confirmed in her refolution to depart, looked as if fhe would exprefs her thanks, when Walfingham, who
appeared already to have acquired the art
of reading her thoughts, faid, " And do
not, I befeech you, Madam, imagine that,
by my undertaking this, you will be under
the leaft obligation to me : far otherwife,
believe me—for you will confer the greateft
of poffible obligations on a man, to whom
life has no longer any value, but what
he can derive from being ferviceable to
others."

Rofalie now thought herfelf perfectly
juftified in accepting an offer which threatened no inconvenience to the ftranger,
while it promifed to reftore her to liberty, and, perhaps, to felicity. Difmif-
fing then all the objections, which ftill
attempted to obtrude themfelves on her
mind, fhe entered into a difcuffion of the
beft means of efcaping from a place, where
the

the few precautions, that were taken to
fecure her ftay, arofe merely from the fuppofed impracticability of her flight.

After a long converfation it was agreed,
that however defirable it might be for her
to go by land, yet fhe would incur great
rifk of being purfued, and in fuch roads
muft inevitably be overtaken.——Nothing therefore remained but for her to
accept what Mr. Walfingham very earneftly offered, in the name of his friend the
Chevalier de Montagny, a conveyance in
the Maltefe galley to any port from whence
it was poffible a paffage to England could be
the moft quickly obtained; Walfingham
affuring her that the veffel and its com-
mander would be entirely at her orders.

This point being fettled, it was next
to be confidered how and when fhe could
leave her prifon with the leaft probability of detection. This was not difficult; but aware, from paft experience, of
the many inconveniences which muft be
encountered at fea, it was neceffary that
what baggage fhe had fhould go with her,
fhe

fhe reminded Walfingham that fhe could not convey this herfelf, nor could fhe even carry it from her room to the lower part of the houfe, without hazarding a difcovery. After a moment's confideration he obviated this objection, by telling her, that as, from her defcription, the caftle was very large, and that there were only two fervants and a peafant who flept there, nothing was more eafy than to introduce a failor, or more, if more were requifite, who would probably be able to pafs through the houfe unnoticed, and convey away whatever fhe wifhed to have with her. He added, " and I will come with them myfelf to prevent all accidents from rafhnefs or blunders. There is a moon, about two o'clock, which will afford us light enough; it is an hour when your keepers will be afleep, and there can be no difficulty in your then leaving a houfe fo flightly guarded."

Rofalie now recollected that there was a very material one—that of the doors being always fhut of a night with great circumfpection, circumfpeĉion, at leaſt fo fhe imagined, becauſe fhe had frequently heard Cattina, after fhe had left her of a night, go round all that part of the building adjoining the great ſtaircaſe, up which the diſtant noiſe of fhutting and barring the maſſive doors founded in fullen echoes. She had often liſtened, after all had been ſtill, for fome moments, and believed that fhe heard the fame precautions taken in the more re- mote parts of the edifice; parts, indeed, where fhe had never been.

When fhe communicated this to Mr. Walſingham, he became impatient.—" If the doors are not eaſily opened, (cried he), we will cut them down; nay, rather batter them with three or four eight pounders, from our galley, than fail."— Rofalie turned pale at the very mention of any expedient of this kind.—Ah, no! (faid fhe); if my efcape cannot be ef- feĉted without the hazard of fhedding blood, I muſt refign myfelf to my de- plorable deſtiny—for I had rather periſh here than be the cauſe of one man's death.

Ah!

Ah! Sir, you do not confider, that, by the leaft alarm given from the caftle, the village below, as well as another higher up the country, would, in an inftant, fend forth their inhabitants ; befide there are arms kept in a lower room, which Cattina once fhewed me, and a fubterraneous communication with the cannon you fee without."——Walfingham fmiled at the formidable phalanx her fancy had thus embodied, well affured that a very few refolute men would put to flight not only the inhabitants of the caftle, but all the peafantry around it who could be collect-ed, and who could have little temptation to rifk their lives in defending the manfion of a woman, whom they had, perhaps, never feen, and to whom they feemed to be very little obliged. Rofalie, how-ever, after paufing a moment, faid fhe recollected, that, on the day when Cat-tina undertook to fhew her where fhe might, perhaps, find fome books, fhe had led her along a paffage adjoining to her bedchamber, and from thence down feveral

veral flights of narrow stairs to the bottom of the building, whence some places, that appeared like arched vaults, led into the room where the papers were deposited, and from thence there was a door opening into the fosse next the garden. She had particularly remarked this door, because Cattina had opened it to give more light to the apartment, which was extremely obscure, from part of it being under ground.—" Cattina (continued she) left me there alone for a considerable time, and when I came out of the room, the door still remained open ; it is therefore probable, that there are no fastenings to it, and that I might go from thence, as well as have my clothes conveyed thither, without alarming Cattina and the other servants, who inhabit quite another part of the house."——Walsingham eagerly seized on this idea, but started a difficulty that had not occurred to Rosalie.—" How (said he) shall we, who are strangers to the castle, find this door, unless we are first shewn it ? "—Rosalie had nothing to propose.

propofe.—"Unlefs, (added her new friend, after a little recolleftion), unlefs I could, before it is dark, go round the caftle, when I think I could eafily difcover the place; there we would wait for you, or, if we found the door open, make our way up, at the hour appointed, to your apart-ment."

To this fcheme, though fhe had nothing better to offer, Rofalie objefted, becaufe fhe dreaded, left the fight of a ftranger fhould raife fufpicions in the fervants; and fhe knew that Cattina, whofe head was filled with ideas of pirates, fince the appearance of one of their xebecs on the coaft, was become more than ufually vigilant in watching, at the windows, if thefe objefts of her terror again appeared.

" What is to be done then, deareft Madam ? (cried Walfingham); we have no time to lofe, and it is abfolutely ne-ceffary that we determine on fomething.— Can you not, from fome place where there is no danger of our being remarked, point out the fide of the building where this

door

door opens into the foffé?"——This appeared the leaft perilous plan, but it was alfo the moft uncertain. Rofalie then led the way, along the fkirts of the wood, to a rifing ground, affording a view of the whole building, and bade Mr. Walfingham remark three tall cyprefles near its weftern extremity.——" If you pafs them, (faid fhe), and walk ftraight on, you will come to what was once a deep foffé immediately furrounding the caftle; but now it is in many places nearly filled up, and the earth and wall are fallen in, infomuch that, when I looked out for a moment at the door in queftion, rather for air than from any curiofity, I perceived I could have got up into the garden by this way."——Walfingham fixed his eyes fteadily on the place, affured Rofalie he fhould not fail to find it; then again repeated, that he would be punctually at the place, with his own fervant and a failor, at two o'clock in the morning, an hour when he knew the moon would afford light to facilitate their

getting

getting on board the veſſel, which would immediately ſail. He inquired, if Roſalie had a watch; ſhe had loſt hers in leaving Sicily; and, therefore, that no miſtake might happen as to the hour, he deſired ſhe would make uſe of one of his, which he ſet by the other.

It now became time to part, for the evening was cloſing in. Walſingham, after a renewal of every proteſtation which was likely to encourage the timid adventurer, whoſe fears and agitation he ſaw painted in her countenance, took a haſty leave, was preſently loſt among the trees, while Roſalie ſlowly returned to her gloomy priſon, dreading leſt any accident ſhould prevent her leaving it; yet trembling at the hazard ſhe muſt incur, and the difficulties ſhe muſt encounter, to regain her liberty.

CHAP.

CHAP. XXVII.

AFTER having given the usual attention to her little boy, Rosalie was at
liberty to make the few arrangements that
were necessary, and to reflect on the step
she was about to take. However earnestly
she had wished for such an opportunity as
was offered her, she trembled now that the
moment approached; yet all she had heard
from Mr. Walsingham, and his zeal, which
did not seem lessened by the knowledge of
her being married, ought to give her
strength of mind and courage. But the
uncertainty of the time of when she should
reach England; the comfortless circumstance of her being so long on board a
vessel, which might be encountered by pirates, where she would be the only woman;
the

the ficknefs and difficulties of fuch a voyage with a little infant; and the doubts how far her hufband might approve of her thus putting herfelf wholly in the power of a ftranger, were confiderations, which, though they did not fhake her refolution, gave dreadful agitation to her fpirits as fhe was about to execute it.

Other fears too affailed her.—The door in the foffé might not be open; fhe was far from being fure fhe could find her way to it; and fhe fhuddered at the thoughts of defcending thefe long and intricate ftair-cafes, and traverfing the vault-like paf-fages leading to the room which fhe was not certain fhe fhould find. Cattina had told her a ftory of a former lord of the caftle, fhe knew not his name, who, being jealous of his wife, had invited the Sig-neur, whom he fufpeded of being in her favour, to an entertainment, when he had killed him, and buried him in fome of thefe rooms, and that lights had often been feen from the loops and windows, and ftrange noifes heard in this end of the

caftle,

caftle, and that nobody had lived in the
lower apartments fince that time. This
was a ftory which had the lefs affected
Rofalie when fhe heard it, becaufe it was
fo common in all old houfes in England
to have fuch a legend. Holmwood had
the ghoft of a lady, in a ruff and farthin-
gale, which always walked on Friday
nights; and fhe was not at all furprifed,
that the old caftle of Formifcufa was fur-
niflhed with the fpirit of a murdered knight:
but now, that it was neceffary for her to
wander alone over the deferted caverns,
which were the fuppofed fcenes of fuch a
tragic adventure, the fame fears and feelings returned as had oppreffed her mind
on the firft two or three days after her arrival in this defolate manfion.

While thefe thoughts paffed in fuccef-
fion through her mind, the hour arrived
for Cattina to bring her evening meal.
Cattina came as ufual, but was not in one
of her beft humours; fhe was fullen and
gloomy, and, inftead of fuch converfation
as fhe fometimes held, fhe feemed difpofed

to

to mutter complaints, though in indirect
and general terms. Rofalie, afraid of her
ftaying, and too confcious of what was
paffing in her own mind, was not able to
command refolution enough to footh and
flatter her into better temper, which fhe
had not unfrequently done. Cattina, however, having fidgetted about the room a
little in her odd way when her temper was
difcompofed, fat down, and a filence enfued, when Rofalie heard the watch in her
pocket, and was ftruck with the fear that
Cattina would hear it too, and knowing
fhe had not one before, would inquire how
fhe came by it; at this idea fhe felt the
blood forfake her cheeks, and was fo
much difcompofed, that, to a more accurate obferver than Cattina, fhe would
undoubtedly have betrayed herfelf.

Cattina, however, who had fome grievances of her own, was fortunately lefs
quick-fighted and intelligent than many
who might have been chofen for the office
of keeper, and after perplexing Rofalie by
a longer ftay than ufual, while fhe talked
and

and made as much noife as fhe could; the female warder of the caftle departed, and, as fhe marched flowly through the adjoining rooms, Rofalie fervently prayed that fhe might never hear thofe founds again.

She now debated with herfelf, whether it would be better to go down firft and examine the door, or wait till the hour when fhe expected Mr. Walfingham to arrive at it, and, after fome deliberation, fhe determined on the former plan, reflecting, that if they came, and found it faftened, the rafhnefs of Mr. Walfingham, who feemed to defpife every danger that could arife from within the caftle, might either impede her flight, or ftain it with fome deed of violence.

It was neceffary, however, to ftay till fhe was fure that Cattina, and the two fervants who belonged to the caftle, were retired for the night; and indeed fhe dreaded the expedition too much to anticipate its execution. She endeavoured, by every argument fhe could draw from

Vol. III.   d   reafon

reafon and religion, to fortify herfelf
againft the fears that affailed her, and, for
a moment, thought fhe had conquered
them. The appearance of fuch a man as
Mr. Walfingham, at fuch a place as Formifcufa, feemed little lefs than a miracle,
and fhe endeavoured to perfuade her mind
it was the particular interpofition of Heaven in her favour; and that to negleft
fuch an occafion of delivering herfelf from
perpetual confinement, would be ingratitude to the Almighty, as well as contrary
to the duty fhe owed her hufband, her
child, and herfelf. Innocent as fhe was
of all offence towards God or Man, what
had fhe to fear?

Fortifying her mind with thefe reflections, and endeavouring to look beyond
prefent inconveniences, fhe thought upon
the time when fhe fhould be reftored to
Montalbert, and fhould remember all that
now perplexed and oppreffed her only as
a fearful dream.

Liftening attentively to the well-known
founds of fhutting the doors, in the inhabited

habited part of the building, fhe heard
them clofed for the night in the ufual
manner; fhe then went to the window to
fee what was the weather—there was more
wind than common, and fhe faw the old
cypreffes wave in the blaft. From the
fea, on the other fide, the moon that was
to light her on her perilous way was juft
emerging. She addreffed herfelf to Heaven, and implored its proteƈion; and,
confcious of the reƈitude of her intentions, believed that fhe fhould go through
the evening's tafk with refolution.

Her own and her child's clothes were
colleƈed in the trunks. She had dreffed
him ready for the journey before fhe put
him to bed, and he flept undifturbed by
the anxieties that agitated his mother's
breaft, who, having determined not to attempt to fleep, looked continually at the
watch, and thought that time moved more
than ufually flow. It was, however, near
midnight, and, once more colleƈing all
her refolution, fhe determined on ex-
amining the door by which fhe hoped to

efcape.

escape. She opened, not without difficulty, that of her chamber, which led to
the avenues of this lower room, and such
was the violence of the wind that rushed
along the paffages, that had she had a
candle in her hand it muft have been extinguished; she trembled, and. retreating,
shut the door haftily. Warned by this
circumftance, she now confidered what
would be her fituation should the light be
extinguished while she was defcending,
and should she lofe her way among the
many winding paffages which she remembered having feen when she followed
Cattina. The apprehenfion was fearful,
and again her refolution to go down the
ftairs failed her.

She returned to her child, whom she
hoped would fleep till her return, kiffed
him, and, imploring for him the protection of Heaven, tried to regain her courage; but as the dread of being left in
utter darknefs, which the rifing wind gave
her great reafon to fear, was ftill the pre-
dominant idea, she endeavoured to take
                                      fuch

fuch precautions as occurred to her againft
it, and furrounded the candle, fhe was
to carry, with a fkreen of paper, lighting
at the fame time the lamp that hung in the
room: then looking at the watch, and
finding it paft midnight, fhe once more
fummoned all her refolution, and foftly
opening the door that the force of the
guft might be lefs fuddenly felt, fhe advanced along the paffage that went from
her room to the place where another
branched from it, leading to the narrow
winding ftairs. She looked fearfully along
thefe black and apparent endlefs avenues;
the half-obfcured light, lent by her fhaded
candle, ferved, indeed, to make " *darknefs
vifible.*" She feared to look long on the
dreary vacuity, left her imagination fhould
embody forms of its own creation; fhe
reached the ftaircafe, and a ftronger blaft
of wind, gathering here as in a funnel,
threatened to extinguifh her light, which
fhe even held with difficulty. She found
herfelf, however, on the next floor, in a
fort of landing place, from whence other

paffages

paffages led off fhe knew not whither, and fhe ftopped a moment to regain her breath, of which fear had nearly deprived her.

In this paufe, however prone her fancy was to imaginary founds as well as fights of horror, fhe heard nothing but the loud gufts of wind that collected beneath from various openings in the walls, and being confined among narrow-vaulted paffages, groaned in loud gufts, then funk into fullen murmurs. Still Rofalie knew it was but the wind, the fame wind that would probably in a few hours lend its friendly affiftance to waft her to the place from whence fhe might procure a paffage to England. This thought animated her courage; fhe raifed her eyes, and affured herfelf that fhe faw nothing which could give her the leaft alarm; bare and broken walls, and dark avenues, which fhe had no bufinefs to explore, furrounded her: fhe determined then to purfue her way flowly and cautioufly, for the fteps of the fecond flight of ftairs were broken and decayed;

decayed; she advanced, when she was suddenly stopped by a sound, which she thought was that of human voices speaking low—she listened with a beating heart. A gust of wind, more violent than she had yet heard, impeded for a moment her distinguishing any other noise; but, as it died away, she was convinced she heard talking, and that there were two or more voices.—What should this mean?—With a trembling hand she once more took the watch, Walsingham had given her, from her pocket. It was not yet half an hour after twelve, and the appointment was not till two. This noise then could not be occasioned by Walsingham and his people waiting for admittance.—What then should it be?—but that their project was by some accident discovered, and that the agents of Signora Belcastro were waiting to entrap those on whom she depended for her deliverance, and that they would afterwards punish her for attempting to escape; probably by tearing her child

D 4

from

from her, and confining her to fome dun-
geon beneath the caftle. Thefe terrific
ideas deprived her, for a moment, of the
power of moving from the place where
fhe ftood; but fhe had gained recollection
enough to refolve on returning up ftairs,
and fhutting her door, before thefe her
cruel purfuers fhould arrive at it, when
a loud and violent crufh confirmed all
her fears; fhe turned, and, as haftily as
her trembling limbs would carry her, fhe
afcended the ftairs, treading lightly. Almoft immediately fhe heard the footfteps
of fome perfon following her. Her refolution would now have failed entirely,
if the greater fear had not conquered the
lefs; for fhe imagined, that while fhe was
thus abfent, her little infant, whom fhe
had left fleeping in its bed, might be carried away; and that idea was fo much
more dreadful than any thing that could
befal herfelf only, that fhe fprang forward
with unufual fwiftnefs—her candle was
extinguifhed, and fhe had no light to
guide

guide her, yet continued to make her way, where, at another time, fhe would have found it difficult even by day.— The fteps behind were heard more near, and fhe thought the man that followed was but a very little way from her when fhe reached the top of the ftairs; the door of her room, which fhe had left open, was fo ftill, and the lamp that remained burning afforded her light to guide her to it. She ran forward to the bed; her boy was calmly fleeping as fhe had left him; fhe threw her arms round him, and funk, quite exhaufted with fear, by his fide—ftill fenfible, but in terror too great to be fupported.

The man who had fo alarmed her, guided by the fame light, followed her into the room, and approached her. Determined to die, rather than part with her child, fhe fhrieked faintly, and implored inarticulately his mercy......But it was Walfingham himfelf that fpoke to her, conjuring her, in the ftrongeft, yet moft

refpeſtful

refpectful terms, to recollect herfelf, protefting that fhe had nothing to fear, unlefs from delay; fince, from the noife he
had been obliged to make, it was poffible
the people in the caftle might be alarmed.
He briefly accounted for coming fo much
before his time, by telling her, that the
wind rifing, the Chevalier de Montagny
was afraid that the leaft increafe might
compel him to put out to fea; in which
cafe fhe would have loft the chance of
efcaping, as he could not have returned
while it blew from the fame quarter, which
it fometimes did for many weeks; and
that they had, therefore, agreed that it
would be better for them to force the
door, in which they had found no difficulty, and rather to hazard alarming her
for a moment, than not enfure her future fafety.

Rofalie, reftored to herfelf by this reafonable account, now exerted herfelf to
fly for ever from this place of dread,
under the guidance of her generous protector,

tector, who told her two men were below that only waited his signal to fetch
her baggage. This he immediately gave;
and Rofalie, having only to wrap her
little boy in the fame coverings as had
ferved them before, during their long
journey, was inftantly ready with him in
her arms.

Walfingham conducted her carefully
down with her fleeping charge, the two
men following with the trunks. Some
little difficulty occurred in her mounting
the broken foffé on the other fide; but
fhe was light, and naturally alert, and
though fhe ftill trembled from her late
terror, the certainty of being releafed
from her cruel confinement, of which
there now feemed no doubt, lent her
ftrength, with the affiftance of Walfingham's fervant, (for fhe would truft her
child only to Walfingham himfelf), to
conquer this impediment. Her deliverer
then followed, and reftored his charge to
her, and offering her his arm, which fhe
readily accepted, they haftened as much

as

as her ftrength would admit, and, after about an hour's walking, found them-felves on the fhore, where the boat wait-ed that was to carry them on board the Maltefe galley.

CHAP. XXVIII.

THOUGH, on account of the tide, the embarkation was troublefome, and though the furge ran high, as the boat made its way to the fhip, yet Rofalie, who now no longer doubted of her efcape, was unconfcious of inconveniences, which, at another time, would have alarmed her. The moment they were fafely on board the Maltefe veffel, Walfingham expreffed his fatisfaction in a manner that gave Rofalie the moft favourable impreffions of the goodnefs of his heart, and the fincerity of his profeffions; while the Chevalier de Montagny welcomed her with all the politenefs and urbanity, for which military men of a certain age, and of his nation, were once fo juftly efteemed. He entreated her to confider herfelf as

miftrefs

miſtreſs of the ſhip, and aſſured her, that
whatever merit there might be in the original purpoſe of his voyage, there was
infinitely more in being inſtrumental to
the deliverance of ſo fair a captive from
impriſonment; and in anſwer to the mingled thanks and apologies which ſhe attempted to utter, he ſaid that he only did
his duty when he lent what aſſiſtance he
could to his Engliſh friend, for that he
was bound, by his military and religious
oath, to ſuccour the injured and diſtreſſed
in every part of the world. The Chevalier then led her into a ſmall ſtate cabin,
extremely commodious for the ſize of the
ſhip, and aſſured her it was hers till ſhe
was landed wherever Mr. Walſingham
ſhould direct, and about which they were
then going to conſult; that he would only,
direct ſome refreſhment to be brought to
her, and then leave her to repoſe.

Roſalie, who, by the quick ſucceſſion
of fear and hope, had hardly had time to
recollect her ſcattered ſenſes during the
laſt few hours, now looked round her,
and

and faw herfelf in comparative fecurity. Delivered from the power of the unrelenting Signora Belcaftro, in the protection, as fhe believed, of men of honour, and in a way of returning to her country, where fhe affured herfelf fhe fhould meet her hufband, fhe now offered up her acknowledgments to that Power who had miraculoufly interpofed to fave her; her full heart, relieved by prayer and tears, beat lefs tumultuoufly, and, notwithftanding the rolling of the fhip, for the wind ftill continued high, fhe fuffered lefs than fhe had ever done at fea before; and even flept many hours, awaking much refrefhed in the morning, and able to go upon deck, where, as the fea was now calm, the fails only gently fwelled with a fummer breeze.

Mr. Walfingham and the Chevalier de Montagny both attended her, and fhe very foon learned to confider the one as a father, the other as a brother; for the former was near fifty years of age. Walfingham no longer made thofe fpeeches

expreffive

expreffive of admiration which had given
her fome pain on their firft meeting; he
feemed no more to confider her as a
beautiful young woman, to whom fuch
compliments might be acceptable, but as
a wife, whom he was reftoring to her
hufband; as a mother, whom he had
preferved for her child. Since he knew
fhe was married, fhe was to him but as a
fifter; and, indeed, he now repeated, that
all his affctions were buried with the
amiable Leonora he had loft, and whofe
death he yet deplored in terms fo pathetic, that. as fhe liftened to him, the foft
eyes of Rofalie were frequently filled with
tears.

The fecond day after they were on board,
and as foon as Rofalie feemed quite recovered from the fright and fatigue that fhe had
fuffered the night fhe quitted Formifcufa,
Walfingham took occafion to tell her, that
he had confulted with the Chevalier de
Montagny, who fubmitted to him at what
port in the Mediterranean they would be
landed; and that he had fettled it fhould
be

be at Marfeilles, whither they were now making their way with a favourable wind. To this Rofalie had nothing to object. Wherever there feemed the greateft certainty of an immediate paffage to England appeared to her the moft eligible; and fhe heard with pleafure, fuch as fhe had long been a ftranger to, that, if the wind continued as favourable as it now feemed to promife, they fhould be at Marfeilles in two or three days.

In the mean time, though the dread of having been too fanguine as to the fate of Montalbert, fometimes obtruded itfelf upon her mind, fhe endeavoured to appeafe thefe fears; and when fhe had once found courage to relate to her two new friends the circumftances under which they had been feparated, fhe received confolation in hearing their opinions that Montalbert was fafe; and when doubts and apprehenfions, as to where he might be, tormented her, Walfingham bade her recollect how eafily fhe might from Marfeilles make inquiry at Naples, and, if he

was

was in Italy, inform him of her health
and refidence. What was to become of
her till all this could be done made now
no part of her uneafinefs; for fhe hoped
and believed the dear mother fhe had left in
England was ready, if not to acknowledge
her as her daughter, to receive her as her
niece, for her marriage with Montalbert
could no longer be a fecret. To Charles
Vyvian alfo, and to William Leffington,
fhe thought it might now be told; and
to the former fhe believed the knowledge
of it would render her as dear as if their
nearer relationfhip was known.

While thefe hopes foothed the folitary
hours of Rofalie, her converfations with
Walfingham impreffed her every moment
with greater refpect for his character, and
pity for the dejection he frequently feemed to feel. He feldom fpoke of himfelf;
but fhe found, from his general converfation, that, in the poffeffion of an af-
fluent fortune, he had no other fatisfaction than as it afforded him the means
of beftowing individual benefits on his
friends,

friends, or affifting, with general benevolence, the unfortunate of every defcription.
While he was thus engaged, the heavy
preffure, which early difappointment had
laid on his heart, feemed to be lightened.
When neither of thefe objects happened
to be immediately within his reach, his
fpirits were extremely unequal; fometimes he was apparently carelefs and gay,
talked of the purfuits which ufually oc-
cupy men of his age with indifference;
threw fome degree of ridicule on the importance fo frequently affixed to them;
and declared himfelf a philofopher, a ci-
tizen of the world, who never meant to
fix himfelf to any country, or any plan of
life; and Rofalie obferved with concern,
that, after thefe efforts, of what fhe could
not but confider as forced and artificial
fpirits, he fometimes funk into the deepeft
dejection; when filent, abfent, and with
a countenance where melancholy and regret were ftrongly expreffed, he appeared
rather to fuffer life than to enjoy it. He
had general and brilliant talents, a mind
highly

highly cultivated, and a taſte elegant and correct. There was no ſcience to which he was a ſtranger, and every European language was familiar to him. Young as he was, he had ſeen a great deal of the world; and he had not merely ſeen it as it appears to a man of fortune, for his devolved to him by the death of an uncle and an elder brother; but was perfectly qualified to judge of the different receptions given by that world to a young man who has his way to make in it, or one who poſſeſſes a large independent fortune. This knowledge had matured his judgment, without narrowing his heart. The variety of countries he had viſited, and the characters he had ſtudied, rendered his converſation extremely entertaining; for, when his ſpirits were really good, it was enlivened by flaſhes of wit, or by anecdotes well told. In his moſt melancholy hours he would ſeek the company of Roſalie, and engage her inſenſibly in converſation, which naturally turned on Montalbert.

Of.

Of an evening, as they fat on the deck together, this fort of difcourfe fometimes continued till Rofalie melted into tears, and till, her fears awakened and encouraged by thus recounting them, fhe deplored Montalbert as if certain of his death, while Walfingham, inftead of attempting, as he had often done, to diffipate her apprehenfions, wept too. The tears flowly ftealing down his cheeks, till fuddenly ftarting, he would feem to recollect the weaknefs, and indeed cruelty, towards Rofalie, of indulging and encouraging fuch emotions, and haftily bidding her good night, would hurry to the cabin of De Montagny.

This refpectable man, who had conceived a fincere affection for his Englifh friend, had, when Rofalie was firft mentioned to him, imagined, that Walfingham had met with fome fair adventurer, and was, according to the ufual morality of his country, extremely willing to affift him in taking advantage of fuch a meeting; but when he faw Rofalie, and had con-

verfed

verfed with her, he was convinced that
he had formed a wrong opinion, and began to be apprehenfive left such an acquaintance fhould have ferious confequences for his friend. When he did
not make a third in their converfations,
he judged of what had paffed by the
manner of Walfingham after them. The
third or fourth day of their voyage, which,
for want of wind, was lengthened beyond
what he had expected, he took occafion
to afk Walfingham, very ferioufly, what
he meant to do with his fair countrywo-
man?

"What I mean to do with her? (replied Walfingham)..... Nay but, my dear
Sir, what a queftion is that?—To reftore
her certainly to her friends in England—
to this happy Montalbert, if he be living!"

"If you do fo, my friend, (faid De
Montagny), let your name be enrolled by
the fide of Scipio's, for affuredly your
merit will be as great."

"Not at all!—Scipio was enchanted by
the beauty of his captive, or there would
have

have been no merit in reftoring her to her lover. Now I am not enchanted with the beauty of Mrs. Montalbert, fuperior as I acknowledge it to be to that of moft women I have feen; therefore I fhall have no merit in acting by her, as I ought, indeed, to act, even if I *were* enamoured of her. But you know, Chevalier, that to me the moft lovely women are become mere objects of admiration, like the pictures and ftatues of Italy."

"Indeed I do not know, nor can I believe any fuch thing, my friend.—For example, I know not how to imagine, that, if this lady had been an antiquity, fuch as you profeffed to fearch for among the ruins of Formifcufa, that you would have ftormed the caftle for her relief."

"It would not have been neceffary; but in fact it is begging the queftion, for had not the lady been young and handfome, fhe would never have been imprifoned there. However, Chevalier, I truft that any woman in diftrefs would have commanded my fervices, as I am fure fhe

would

would yours, merely becaufe fhe was a diftreffed woman."

" *My* fervices are dedicated, you know, to the diftreffed of every defcription ; but to damfels in trouble I can be confidered of little more importance than their con-feffors when once my fervice is ended, for I am but a kind of military monk : but you, my good friend, at the age of three or four and twenty, are, perhaps, a protector for a very young and very pretty woman, who might be lefs excep-tionable in Italy, than among Meffieurs les Anglais."

" You do not fuppofe then (faid Wal-fingham) that Montalbert can be fuch a fool, or fuch a brute, as to be difpleafed that his wife has put herfelf under my protecton to efcape from the tyranny of his mother ?"

" Oh, no !—(replied De Montagny) ; I fuppofe nothing......I only fear, that being continually with fuch a woman as Madame de Montalbert ; hearing from thofe beautiful lips, profeffions of grati-tude,

tude, and gazing on thofe charming eyes, filled with tears of tendernefs, it may prove, at laft, a very fevere trial to my friend's fortitude, when the hour fhall come in which he muft give her back to this happy Montalbert."

" Would to Heaven that were to hap-pen to-morrow, (anfwered Walfingham, clafping his hands, and fpeaking with warmth)—would to Heaven it might be to-morrow that I could fee her happy!"

" I wifh it were, (faid De Montagny drily) ; but if, when the time is paft, you can inform me that you really felt, as you now believe you fhall *then* feel, I may then proclaim my friend the moft extra-ordinary man of his age in the three king-doms of his mafter."

" I verily believe I fhall claim your eulogium, De Montagny, and I here pro-mife honeftly to relate to you what paffes in my heart at that time......Ah! (added he, with a deep-drawn figh), you have no conception, my dear Chevalier, of the hold that fuch an attachment, as mine, to

VOL. III.   E   a lovely

a lovely woman, who is now no more, has on the heart.—I fay, *you* can have no idea of it, becaufe, defigned from your early youth for the Order of Malta, you never allowed yourfelf to form fuch attachments as were at all ferious; but *I* feel it to be impoffible ever to love another, and all my hopes of felicity are buried in the grave of my Leonora."

" All that is very well. I am fure you now think what you fay ; but—we have read, and even feen, certain events, that difpofe me to believe much in the influence of time and defpair, as remedies for thefe violent paffions.......... In fhort ---------"

" In fhort! (interrupted Walfingham); you don't believe the paffion can exift when the objeð is no more ?"

" I believe it is *transferable*, my friend, if not curable: I have feen—oh! I know not how many inftances of it......... You have read perhaps, or, perhaps, you have feen a little after-piece, on the French ftage, called Le Veuf ?"

" Oh!

"Oh! (exclaimed Walfingham impatiently), if we were to give up every fentiment as ridiculous, that your writers, or your dramatifts, attempt to render fo, there would not be left, in the human heart, one virtue to reconcile us to the mifery of exiftence."

De Montagny, who meant not to hurt his friend, feeing that he took the matter more ferioufly than was intended, let the converfation drop, and Walfingham, whofe fpirits were much agitated, went upon deck, where the ftars reflected in the clear expanfe of a fea fo perfectly calm, that the veffel did not perceptibly move; the ftillnefs of the night, fcarcely difturbed by the flow rippling of the waves parted by its prow, and the mildnefs of the air, reftored him to a more tranquil ftate. He bade the fteerfman and a boy, who was on the firft watch, begin the evening hymn fung by the Maltefe failors. He fat down on the gunwale, and bore a part; the tumult of his fpirits entirely fubfided,

and

and he began to wonder how they had
been fo difturbed!—" But it provokes
me, (faid he, as he reflected on the matter)—it provokes me, that a man of fuch
good fenfe, and fo excellent a heart,
fhould adopt prejudices fo entirely the
refult of the manners of his country, and
his own particular mode of education. ....
How *can* he, with fentiments fo generally
honourable, believe that I could fuffer
myfelf to feel, for this charming woman,
any other degree of tendernefs than might
be infpired by an amiable fifter?—No!—
to fuppofe me capable of other views, is
to deftroy the pleafure I take in protecting and ferving her ; and why would he
rob me of the only happinefs I am now
capable of tafting?—In love with Mrs.
Montalbert, or in danger of becoming
fo!—Good God! how can he think fo?—
When I fee her, I am calm and contented; when my heart throbs with recollected anguifh, I hear her voice, and forget that I am miferable. She fpeaks of
her

her husband, and I weep with her; she caresses her child, and I weep still more! If I loved her, the name of this husband would be hateful to me, and I should be jealous even of her maternal affection. . . . . Alas! I know I have severely learnt what love is, and I am sure the sensations I now feel have nothing to do with it."

As if, however, Walsingham, convinced of this himself, was conscious of the propriety there was in Rosalie's knowing it too, he now took every occasion when they were alone, and still more particularly when the Chevalier de Montagny was with them, to speak in stronger terms than ever of his widowed affections; and that he considered himself as wedded to the memory of his adored Leonora.—— Rosalie seemed to hear him with mingled emotions of compassion and regard; she pitied the anguish he felt, and respected the constancy of his affection. He repeated one of the tenderest sonnets of Petrarch, and then an imitation of it, which he had written; and Rosalie, not-

with-

withstanding the advantage the Italian language gives to this species of compofition, preferred Walfingham's imitation. De Montagny, an unprejudiced fpectator of thefe fcenes, faw that Rofalie's heart was at prefent fecure; but he every day fancied he had more reafon to tremble for that of his friend.

At length, after being twice the time they had calculated on their paffage, they landed at Marfeilles. Walfingham fecured a lodging for Rofalie in the moft retired part of the town, where he hired a female fervant to attend her, and he went himfelf to an hotel. Her heart thanked him for this delicacy; nor was fhe lefs fenfible of the kindnefs of the Chevalier de Montagny, who, purely from motives of friendfhip to Walfingham, and of compaffion to her, had taken a voyage of-fome length, and attended to her the whole time with as much good-nature and humanity as if he had been her neareft relation. It was, therefore, with infinite regret that fhe bade him farewel, when, three days after her arrival

rival at Marſeilles, he waited on her, with Walſingham, and told her his ſhip was then taking up its anchors, and that, in the evening, he ſhould go on board, and get under weigh for Malta.

CHAP. XXIX.

THE port of Marfeilles was crowded
with Englifh veffels, for, after a war,
trade fuddenly revives. Walfingham, therefore, had his choice of conveyances by
fea; but he doubted whether he ought
not to propofe to Rofalie making the journey by land to Calais. Long accuftomed
to travel, the method of going from place
to place was indifferent to him, and his
choice was ufually determined by the op-
portunities offered of feeing fome object
worth notice that had not before fallen
within his obfervation. As he had paffed
three times from the fouth of France to
England, and every time by a different
route, he had no curiofity to gratify, even
if his attention to Rofalie had allowed him,

in

in the prefent inftance, to think of any other object in his way.

When, therefore, he bade adieu to his friend De Montagny, which lowered and deprefled his fpirits extremely, he walked to the lodgings of Rofalie, who had all day expected him, for De Montagny had taken leave of her the day before, and fhe imagined him gone. New alarms had poffeffed her, on the reafonablenefs of which fhe wifhed to have confulted Walfingham, but it was evening before he came, and then with fo dejected an air, and a countenance fo melancholy, that Rofalie fancied fome new difafter, fhe knew not what, had overtaken them, and was afraid to afk. Walfingham, however, told her, that, believing it to be her wifh to reach England as expeditioufly as poffible, he was come to hear her commands on that fubject; the whole purpofe of his prefent vifit being to know how and when fhe would depart.

" Alas! Sir, (replied fhe, hurt, yet hardly confcious that fhe was fo, at fome-

thing

thing in his manner which appeared unufual)——Alas! Sir—I know fo little of
travelling, or of the advantages or difadvantages of different roads, or different
conveyances, that I muft refer myfelf entirely to you. I only know, that the method which would be the leaft troublefome
to you, would, on that account, be the
moft agreeable to me — — — — — —." Her
voice faltered. " Yet there is one ap-
prehenfion (added fhe) that I have to-day
been taught to entertain, which has extremely alarmed me. I am told that the
fmall-pox, of a malignant fort, is at Marfeilles—if my child — — — —."

Walfingham immediately comprehended
what fhe would fay. " I intended (faid
he) to have mentioned to you, what, I
find, fome perfon has anticipated; it will
undoubtedly be a reafon for you to haften
from hence. I have, I believe, often
told you, dear Madam, (added he, lowering and foftening his voice), that I have
no ufe for the fortune I poffefs, but that
of affifting my friends..... Alone upon this
earth,

earth, with no very near relations, nor any diftant ones who want my affiftance, there are no claims on my property, to me a great part of it is ufelefs—you would give it value by ufing it. After fuch a declaration you will not fuppofe that the difference of expence, between a journey by fea or land, ought to be a confideration. There would even be an indelicacy in my naming the fubject, had you not once or twice talked of expence. There is then only to confider, whether you prefer going by fea to England, or travelling acrofs France to Calais, or any other ports; confult your own eafe and fafety, and that of your dear little boy."

Rofalie, ftill unable to decide, and ftill more unable to exprefs what fhe felt of obligation to him, was filent for fome moments, and then referred herfelf again to him. At length, having weighed the fatigue of a very long journey by land, againft the poffible delays by fea, for there was hardly any *danger* to be named at fuch a feafon of the year, it was agreed

that

that Walfingham fhould engage their paffage in the moft commodious fhip he could
find; and though Rofalie, who dreaded
nothing fo much as being troublefome to
her benefactor, expreffed but little of the
anxiety fhe fuffered about her child, Walfingham underftood her, and, without faying he fhould do fo, he took care to hire
a veffel in which there was a furgeon and
a ftock of medicines. It had lately been
engaged to bring over an Englifh nobleman for the recovery of his health, and
the accommodations and medical attend-
ant, which had been engaged for him,
feemed moft fortunately at hand for Rofalie. The price demanded Walfingham
gave at once, with a farther fum on condition that the captain fhould immediately depart, without waiting for any other
paffengers. Money is fo forcible an ad-
vocate, that the captain was convinced it
was his intereft to comply with this requeft,
and every thing was foon ready.

In little more than a week from her
landing at Marfeilles, Rofalie embarked

for

for England, having written from thence
to Naples, and enclofed her letter to Montalbert to the Englifh Minifter.

During a very profperous voyage Walfingham behaved to her with the affection
of a brother; but as they had now loft
the fociety of the Chevalier de Montagny,
who ufed, with great propriety, to break
their too-frequent tête-à-têtes, Walfingham lived more in his own cabin than he
had done when they were on board the
Maltefe veffel, and was, or affected to be,
engaged in the ftudy of Arabic, in which
language he had purchafed fome curious
manufcripts at Marfeilles. When thefe
ftudies happened to be the fubject of his
converfation with Rofalie, he faid he was
making himfelf acquainted with Arabic,
becaufe, having already vifited almoft every
part of Europe, he thought his next voyage
would be to Afia. He frequently repeated this before the captain and the doctor,
as they called, a furgeon's mate who was
on board, and they, as well as the failors,
who heard the fame thing from Walfingham's

ham's fervant, could not but wonder that
fuch a young man, who was happy enough
to have fo very pretty a woman belong
to him, fhould be of fo reftlefs a difpofition. That Rofalie was his miftrefs they
none of them at all doubted, notwithftanding his referved and refpectful behaviour
towards her; but he was too rich and
too generous for them to make fuch
remarks, as they would certainly have
indulged themfelves in, had their paffengers been of inferior fortune.

Though to fee England had been the
firft wifh of Rofalie's heart ever fince the
miferable day that drove her from Sicily,
though fhe knew all her friends fhe had
on earth were to be found there, and
though fhe had perfuaded herfelf fhe
fhould meet Montalbert there, yet, as fhe
approached it, her anxiety became ex-
ceffive; and when the man at the maft
head cried Land! as they entered the
Channel, her heart beat, as if, in a few
moments, her deftiny was to be decided.
Now like clouds, doubtful and indiftinct,
the

the white cliffs rofe above the horizon;
and now they gradually became more vifible, till, at length, from the deck were
difcerned thofe towering boundaries of
the coaft; which——

" Confpicuous many a league, the mariner
" Bound homeward, and, in hope, already there,
" Greets with three cheers exulting !!! "

COWPER.

Rofalie gazed at them with eyes filled with
tears, and filently demanded—" Is Montalbert there?—Ah! do the friends—the
few friends that love me, yet exift?"—
While Walfingham, though from different
motives, feemed to be affected in the fame
manner, he, alas! knew, that England
held only the afhes of her whom he had
loved; but though tempted to fay——

" Sento l'aura mia anlica; e i dolci colli
" Veggio apparir onde'l bel lume naeque
" Che tenne gli occhi miei, mentr'al ciel piaque
" Bramofi, e lieti; or li tien trifti, e molli
" O caduche fperanze, o penfier folli I
" Vedove l'erbe, e torbido fon l'acque: &c."

PETRARCH.

Yet,

Yet, amidſt this natural and juſt regret,, which he had hitherto been proved to nouriſh, he was conſcious that, if when they went on ſhore, he was to take leave of Roſalie, he ſhould feel a new deprivation, which would make all his wounds bleed afreſh.

This ſentiment, however, he ventured not to communicate to her, nor had he ever yet found courage to aſk her what were her intentions, or how ſhe meant to diſpoſe of herſelf after they landed at Falmouth, where he had engaged the ſhip to put them aſhore ?—When within an hour's ſail, with trembling and heſitation, which he vainly endeavoured to conquer, he at laſt inquired to what part of England ſhe meant to go ?

Roſalie, though ſhe had conſidered this before, had never ſteadily thought on what would be her beſt plan to purſue. Since, however, as it was now neceſſary to determine on ſomething, ſhe ſaid ſhe would wait wherever ſhe landed, or in the neareſt convenient town, till ſhe could receive

letters

letters from Mrs. Vyvian, to whom she
meant immediately to write, under cover
to Mrs. Leffington, the only means by
which she could be fure of a letter
reaching her. The heart of Rofalie funk
when she recollected the ftate of health
in which she had left her mother, and
when her mind ran back to the many
months of her abfence, she trembled to
reflect on what might, in fuch an interval,
have been the confequence of that injured health, and of, perhaps, increafing
anxiety. All her hopes were centered in
her mother; from her only she could receive protection and comfort—from her
only obtain information of Montalbert;
till, therefore, she could hear of Mrs. Vyvian, she could herfelf form no fettled
plan.

She related as much to Walfingham as
appeared neceffary to account for her remaining in whatever part of England she
landed, till she had anfwers to the letters
she should write immediately on her arrival. He obferved to her, that it would
then

then be much better for her to be at an
eafier diftance from London, and propofed that, inftead of landing at Falmouth,
he fhould engage the captain to go on to
Portfmouth, for which the wind was extremely favourable. Rofalie readily af-
fented; fince fhe fhould in that country
be very near the place which fhe once
confidered as her home. One of thofe,
whom fhe had believed her fifter, was
an inhabitant of Chichefter, another refided not far from thence; and though
fhe felt no inclination to appear before
thefe her relations, while her fituation
was liable to mifinterpretations, yet there
was fomething confoling in the reflection
that fhe fhould be within reach of fome
perfons fhe knew, and who could have
no reafon, when they were informed fhe
was the wife of Mr. Montalbert, to be
otherwife than proud of the connection.

The fame fears that had difturbed Rofalie at Marfeilles, for the health of her
infant boy, affailed her when fhe landed
with him at Portfmouth. There was no
refource

fource for that evening but an inn; this
and many other confiderations induced
her to wifh to quit the town as foon as
poffible; and now fhe thought with confufion and anguifh of mind, which had
been lefs felt while they were both citizens
of the world, that fhe was entirely dependent for fubfiftence on the friendfhip
of Walfingham, to whom fhe was already
but too much obliged. How could fhe
reconcile this to pride, or to propriety ?
Yet there was no remedy; for till fhe
could receive anfwers from Mrs. Vyvian,
what refource had fhe?—The conduct of
Mr. Walfingham had been delicate and
generous; the more fhe was unavoidably
in his power, the more referved he became. But though fhe knew her own innocence, and was affured of his honour,
fhe could not recollect, without apprehenfion, that fhe was now in her native country; that fhe had quitted it without daring
to avow her marriage, and had fince been
loft to all her former connections; that
fhe now muft appear in a very equivocal
                              character,

character, and that few would liften to, and fewer ftill believe, an account of the extraordinary circumftances that had brought her into her prefent fituation. Circumfcribed, as was her knowledge of the world, fhe had feen enough of it to know that a very moderate fhare of beauty excites the envy of every woman who has lefs, and that there are crowds of goffip-ping people, to whom fuch a ftory, as her's appeared to be, would afford the higheft gratification, and from whom it might ex-cite the moft cruel remarks.

To hide herfelf, therefore, from the eyes of curiofity and malevolence, till fhe could appear properly acknowledged and protected, ought certainly to be her de-termination ; but whither fhould fhe go, and by whom fhould fhe be guided?—It was not poffible for her to communicate to Walfingham the painful fenfations thefe reflections brought with them ; but he faw them in her eyes, in her manner, and he heard them in the tremulous accents of her voice—yet he knew almoft as little as.

fhe.

She did how to begin a converfation which every moment rendered more neceffary. He fat looking at her, as fhe was writing to Mrs. Vyvian and Mrs. Leffington, confidering what he ought to fay, when, having finifhed her letters, Rofalie laid down the pen, and faid, in a half-whifper, " And whither fhall I tell my friends to direct their anfwers?"——— This, though rather a foliloquy than an addrefs to Walfingham, gave him occafion to fay, " You will determine, dear Madam, whither you like to go......You will recollect, I hope, that I have only to obey you, and --------;" he hefitated—Rofalie, fpeaking faintly, interrupted him.

" If I knew (faid fhe) any village near this place --------."

" I mean not to dictate, (cried Walfingham, recovering himfelf). If you have no particular reafons for wifhing to be near Portfmouth, I think any, indeed almoft every, fituation equally within reach of London,

London, and of a daily poſt from thence, would be preferable. I have heard you ſpeak of having once lived in the neighbourhood of Chicheſter; it is at an eaſy diſtance from hence, and - - - - - -."

" Oh! no—(ſaid Roſalie), not Chicheſter—I cannot go thither. . . . . . . I do not (continued ſhe) wiſh to have it known there that I am in England till - - - - -."

Walſingham did not give her time to finiſh the ſentence, but ſaid, " Would you then like to go nearer London, or to ſome retired place on the ſea coaſt, where, at this ſeaſon, there will be very few people, and where you may meet with accommodations, in regard to lodgings, which country towns do not afford ? "

" That would certainly be the moſt eligible, (replied Roſalie). I have no wiſh to approach London, (added ſhe ſighing), till I know what hope there is of my meeting there, or at leaſt hearing there of, Mr. Montalbert."

" Have

" Have you ever visited any of these villages on the coast ? (inquired Walsingham) ;—Is there one you prefer?"

" I was once at Eastbourne, (answered she, and it was at this time of the year. I remember thinking the country around it extremely pleasant, and there was then no company, or only one or two invalids."

" I know the place, (said Walsingham), and I believe you cannot fix better. It is necessary to determine, because you must give your friends your address before the post goes out."

" I will say then, that at the post-office at Eastbourne my letters are to be left.— But—I cannot help feeling uneasy that the wife of Mr. Montalbert should appear ; perhaps I am wrong, Sir—but my situation is a very delicate one...... I could wish my real name were not known till my family owns me -----" she stopped ; but Walsingham saw she meant more than she had courage to utter.——" My dear Madam, (said he), that is a matter on
which

which I cannot even give my opinion;
your own good fenfe muft decide upon it.
You will determine, (faid he, getting up
and leaving the room), and when you
have done fo, I will fet out myfelf to
fecure your accommodations, as I conclude you will go from hence as early as
you can."

Left then to decide for herfelf, and
having very little time to do fo, fhe haftily
refolved to drop her own name till fhe
heard from her mother, and requefted
that the anfwers fhe folicited might be
enclofed to Mrs. Sheffield, (the firft name
that occurred to her), to be left at the poft-
office Eaftbourne. Having fealed and fent
out her letter, Walfingham returned. He
heard what fhe had done, and then faid,
that as fhe might now travel in perfeft
fecurity, attended only by a fervant, he
would, with her permiffion, go on firft,
befpeak poft-horfes on the road, and procure her lodgings at the place fhe had
fixed upon—adding, " I will give proper
direftions to Waters, (his fervant), fo that
you

you will have no trouble, and, I hope, not much fatigue......You will fleep on the road!"

" If you think it neceffary, (anfwered Rofalie); but I do not recollect the diftance, nor the ftages, having never travelled along the coaft. It will not be neceffary, I fuppofe, to fleep at Chichefter?"

. Walfingham anfwered that he thought Brighthelmftone would be preferable, and then faid, " I fhall fee you on Saturday at Eaftbourne, I hope in health and fafety; and afterwards (continued he, half-fuppreffing a figh) I fhall—that is, you know, I *muft* take my leave, and once more, unlefs I can be of any farther ufe to you, become a diffipated wanderer, feeking for fomething that may fupply the place of happinefs."

Then, without ftaying to hear thofe thanks which Rofalie endeavoured to utter, he departed, and in about a quarter of an hour Waters came to her with a letter, which he told her his mafter, who was gone, had left for her. The man then defired to know at what hour the next morning fhe would be pleafed to have the chaife ready, and, having received her orders, went away, leaving her to perufe her letter.

CHAP. XXX.

LETTER.

THERE are a thousand occasions in
life, in which I feel that writing is better
than speaking. When either the person
I am speaking to, or the matter I am
speaking upon, interests me greatly, I am
the worst orator in the world; and, therefore, my fair fellow traveller, I write to
you, for you must be convinced that I
am deeply concerned for you and for your
future happiness.

Though I have not the pleasure of
being acquainted with Mr. Montalbert,
yet I will flatter myself that, when we
meet, I shall find in him another friend.

He

He muſt be generous, amiable, and can-
did, for he is beloved by Roſalie; but as
we know not when he will return, and
as I am, according to the opinion of the
world, too young for a guardian, we muſt—
ah! how cruel a neceſſity!—ſubmit to the
rigid ordinances of prudence; and, though
I own to you that I ſhall relinquiſh the
greateſt pleaſure of my life when I leave
you, yet I mean to remain no longer at
the village, whither you are going, than
to ſee you ſettled. This, I know, is what
I ought to do, ſince, however diſintereſted my regard for you may be, the world
is too uncandid, and too little refined, to
give me credit for poſſeſſing ſuch ſenti-
ments. You are infinitely amiable, and
I am probably allowed no more virtue
than other young men, though I hope and
I think I have never deſerved the character of a libertine..... All this, my dear
Madam, you could not ſay to me, but I
know you have thought it. Half my acquaintance would laugh at *me* for ſaying it,
but

but I am accuftomed to do what I know
to be right, and to difregard every kind of
cenfure which is not incurred by actions
really bad.

With this turn of mind, and after what
I have faid, you will believe that I would
not propofe any fcheme, merely to gratify
myfelf, which fhould break in upon the
regulations that feem neceffary for your
fake; nor will I, without your approba-
tion, execute that I have in view. A
friend of mine has a houfe at Haftings,
whither he goes with his family for a
month or two in the autumn, the only
time when his engagements at the bar allows him to be abfent from London. I
once paffed a few days with him there, and
I am on that footing of intimacy which
allows me to afk for the ufe of his houfe.
He knows that I am an unfettled itinerant,
and will not be furprifed at my fudden
appearance in England, although he has
loft fight of me for eighteen or twenty
months, and believes me either in Spain,

F 3   Portugal,

Portugal, or Italy ; I fhall tell him (what
is true) that I am come home for a fhort
time; that it is not convenient for me to
be fo far from London as at my own
houfe in the weft; and that this, united
with a wifh of being retired, are my reafons for borrowing his houfe at Haftings :
I fhall be within fuch a diftance as to have
continually the power of learning how and
when I may be ferviceable to you.....
Will you then give me your permiffion to
remain there?—My vifits to Eaftbourne
fhall be regulated by your orders, and
furely the moft vigilant and cenforious
prudery cannot object to the friendly and
unfrequent vifits of a brother to a fifter.
Oh! would you were really my fifter,
with what delight fhould I then avow the
intereft I take in your happinefs; fuppofe
yourfelf to be fo, I entreat you, and honour me by accepting the enclofed without ever mentioning the fubject, left I
fhould doubt your honouring me with that
efteem as to allow me to ufe the affectionate

tionate names of friend and brother, when
I am permitted to affure you of the regard and efteem of,

  Dear Madam,
   Your moft faithful
    and obliged fervant,
     F. WALSINGHAM.

The enclofure was a bank note of a
hundred and fifty pounds.

Rofalie, whofe tears had fallen, fhe
hardly knew why, while fhe read this letter, could not immediately determine how
fhe ought to anfwer it. She had, it was
true, time enough to confider it on her
journey, but it hung upon her fpirits, and
drove fleep from her eyes. After placing,
however, in every point of view, the intention which he fo delicately afked her
permiffion to execute, fhe thought there
would be not only prudery and ingratitude in refufing her affent, but that it
would fhew a miftruft, which fhe faw as
degrading to herfelf and unjuft towards
him. The money which he fent her gave

       her

her more concern, yet fhe confidered that
it was lefs uneafy to her feelings to receive it in this manner, than to be laid
under the painful neceffity of applying to
him for fmall fums, fhould fhe wait long
for the letters fhe expe&ed, and, till they
arrived, what other refource had fhe ?—
The hope, ever alive in her heart, that
Montalbert would foon return, and grate-
fully repay all the pecuniary favours fhe
owed Walfingham, reconciled her to this
temporary obligation, which fhe knew could
be no inconvenience to him.

In the morning fhe arofe, impatient to
begin her journey, and fent for Waters to
get the note changed in order to pay her
expences ; but he informed her, that it
was already done, and that his mafter had
given him dire&ions for the journey in
the fame manner as when he travelled
himfelf.

Rofalie, her Marfeilloife maid Claudine,
and the obje& of her conftant folicitude,
her child, were placed in a chaife, which
Waters had hired for the whole journey,

to

to avoid the trouble and delay of changing the baggage, and they were very foon at Chicheller. As fhe paffed through that town, and fat at the door of the inn, while the horfes were putting to, a thoufand recollections crowded upon her mind. The objects, formerly fo familiar to her, brought back the days of Rofalie Leffington, and the ftrange viciffitudes that had happened fince feemed rather like the fictions of romance than reality; fhe was then the daughter of a village curate, humbled by her fuppofed fifters, and fhrinking with terror from paternal authority, which feemed likely to compel her to marry a man fhe difliked. Her prefent fituation formed a ftrong contraft to that fhe was then in; but was it better?—She was now the daughter of parents who did not own her, a wife without a hufband, and the mother of an infant who feemed to have been born to misfortunes. While fhe indulged thefe mournful thoughts fhe did not venture to fhew herfelf, left fhe fhould be known; this

precaution

preeaution was fortunate, for juft before the horfes were put to her chaife, her former admirer, Hughfon, mounted on an ungovernable horfe, pranced up to the fide of it. The beaft was impatient to enter the ftable; the chaife in which Rofalie fat was immediately before the gateway of the inn-yard, and Hughfon, ever folicitous to fhew his horfemanfhip, (though he now little thought to whom), fpurred and irritated his horfe; it began to rear and kick with a violence, which, for a moment, made her apprehend fome mifchief to the chaife that might compel her to get out. This fear, however, lafted but a moment; the conteft between the horfe and his rider, the latter of whom feemed much the leaft rational of the two, was ended, at leaft in that fpot, for the former fpringing away with great fwiftnefs was inftantly out of fight, while the boys and people in the ftreet, ftaring after him, exclaimed, " That Parfon Hughfon's horfe had run'd clear away wi un."

Fortunately

Fortunately it was the contrary road to that which Rofalie was going; but the carriage had hardly proceeded ten paces farther before fhe faw Blagham walking with a gentleman of the neighbourhood whom fhe well remembered. She now rejoiced that fhe was going to a diftance from thefe her old acquaintance, whofe notice and intrufion it was improbable fhe could have efcaped had fhe remained at any place within their reach; a confideration which had confirmed her refolution of going into the eaftern part of the county.

The remainder of her journey paffed without any particular occurrence or accident. She often amufed herfelf by calculating the time when it was probable Montalbert would receive the letter which fhe had written to him from Marfeilles; but this depended fo much on circumftances, that there was no date on which her mind could reft with fatisfaction.— The time when fhe might affure herfelf of an anfwer from her real, and her fup-

pofed

pofed, mother, was more eafily afcertained, and to that fhe looked forward
with the hope of having much of her prefent uncertainty and uneafinefs alleviated.
Juft before the chaife mounted the high
down immediately before the village, fhe
faw Walfingham watching for her approach. He did not, however, ftop the
chaife, but gave Waters a direction to the
houfe he had taken, that there might be
no neceffity for her to drive firft to an inn.
Rofalie was prefently fet down at the door
of this houfe, which, though the moft retired, was one of the moft commodious
lodgings in the village ; when her baggage
was taken out, and the chaife difcharged,
Walfingham made his appearance. He
inquired eagerly how fhe found herfelf
after her journey, and how her little boy
was?—then afked, if fhe approved of her
apartments?—He told her dinner was
ready, and folicited leave to dine with
her, adding, that he had a chaife ready to
carry him away as foon as dinner was over.
All this paffed with a rapidity which Rofalie

falie eafily faw was intended to prevent any converfation on the fubject of his letter; and, indeed, fhe had neither courage or inclination to enter upon it at that moment. Dinner was ferved immediately; it paffed in common converfation, Rofalie trying, but not very fuccefsfully, to bear her part. It was hardly over, and the fervant withdrawn, when Waters came in to fay that the chaife, his mafter had ordered, was ready at the inn. Walfingham directed him to put his baggage into it, and wait there till he came; then, turning to Rofalie, he gravely faid——

" And now, dear Madam, it depends upon you to decide whither I fhall go? If you think there is the leaft impropriety in my ftaying fo near you at Haftings, I will direct my courfe to London.... Alas! (added he), no place affords me happinefs; and I have at this time no other purpofe than to contribute what may be in my power to yours."

Rofalie, pained and confufed, knew not what to anfwer. A fenfe of all the obligations

gations fhe owed to this excellent friend
preffed heavily on her mind ; fhe believed
thofe obligations had been conferred with
the moft difinterefted views,, and, cautious
as he feemed to be to avoid every other
interpretation, fhe thought that to infift
on his wholly quitting the country, becaufe fhe refided in it, would be not only
a needlefs and abfurd piece of prudery,
but imply a doubt of his motives; fhe was
confcious too of her unprotected fituation, and could not but be fenfible that
to have this friend within a fhort diftance
was a moft defirable circumftance for her;
neither did fhe imagine, as nothing was
known of her, and but little of him in
this country, that cenfure could find food
for its malevolence in their refiding, perhaps, for a fhort time only, within miles
of each other. After fome hefitation,
therefore, fhe told him, that fuch was her
opinion of his good fenfe, and fuch her
conviction of the real friendfhip he bore
her, that fhe was perfuaded fhe might
leave it entirely to him to act as was moft
agreeable

agreeable or convenient to himfelf; at the fame time fhe took from her pocket the bank note he had enclofed to her, entreating him to allow her to return it.

The conclufion of Rofalie's fpeech feemed to hurt, as much as the beginning of it had gratified, Walfingham.—"Ah! Mrs. Montalbert, (faid he), can you talk of the few fervices I have had the good fortune to render you, and yet mention fuch a trifle as that?—I befeech you do not mortify me, by fuffering any obligation of this nature to dwell on your mind."

Rofalie, however, infifted on giving him an acknowledgment of it in writing, to which he unwillingly confented. He then entreated her to let him know the moment fhe heard from her friends; afked if he might not ride over fome morning about the time fhe expected her letters, as he had fent for his horfes. Having received her affent, and tenderly careffed her little boy, he left her with vifible reluctance, and, going to the inn, threw himfelf into the

the poft-chaife that was to convey him to Haftings.

Rofalie, being now left alone, endeavoured to calm her fpirits, fo long the fport of incertitude and anxiety. Nothing could immediately occur to difturb her tranfient quiet, for it was yet fome days before it was poffible for her to receive the anfwers from Mrs. Leffington, which fhe had fo earneftly folicited. It might even be prolonged, if, as was poffible, Mrs. Vyvian was in the north.

Rofalie found that every thing had been fettled in her new abode, where the people of the houfe were to attend her. The woman was very civil, and feemed to have no curiofity to learn more than fhe had been told of her new lodger, whom Walfingham had reprefented as a young lady, his diftant relation, who was in expectation of her hufband from Italy, and that her ftay at Eaftbourne was uncertain. It might be only a few weeks, or it might be much longer. An uncertainty that afforded

forded a profpect of great advanfage to the landlady, while the liberality, with which her terms had been agreed to, aided the favourable impreffion that could hardly fail to be given by the innocence, beauty, and fweetnefs of Rofalie's countenance and manner.

Claudine, carrying the infant boy, was the conftant companion of her miftrefs's walks, which beguiled the greateft part of every day, and were varied between the green and fhady lanes, open downs, or the immediate borders of the fea. On the fea itfelf Rofalie often fixed her eyes for hours, and her imagination went forth in conjectures about Montalbert, which became lefs and lefs pleafant as time ftole on. From thefe penfive wanderings fhe conftantly returned at the hours when letters were delivered, and impatiently inquired if there were any addreffed to Mrs. Sheffield; but a week wore away, and none arrived; yet it was certain that fhe might have had an anfwer in that time; Walfingham too had reckoned the termination

mination of a week as a period when intelligence was almoſt certain, and he, therefore, availed himſelf of the permiſſion he had received to come over.— Roſalie rejoiced to ſee him, and ſought not to conceal the ſatisfaction it gave her, while he appeared more dejected and melancholy than ſhe had ever yet known. He had now no object in view on which to exerciſe his benevolence; nothing to rouſe him from the deſpondence which ſo frequently obſcured the faculties of his mind; and to this cauſe, Roſalie, who knew from obſervation that he required ſome generous motive for active exertion, attributed the gloom which hung over him.

This heavy depreſſion of ſpirits ſeemed to break away after he had converſed with her an hour or two, and, in proportion as ſhe appeared uneaſy at the delay of Mrs. Leſſington's anſwer, he found reaſons to appeaſe that fiend Inquietude. At length they began to converſe on indifferent ſubjects, and, during their walk

on

on the hill, attended by Claudine, who was always directed to follow them, Walsingham infensibly led the difcourfe to his own hiftory and affairs. He talked of his family, and lamented that he was left an ifolated being in the world. " I have now (faid he) no nearer relation than a coufin of nearly my own age, who inherits a very large fortune from another branch of my family, and from his mother, who was an heirefs; but our difpofitions and our purfuits are fo different, that we never affociate, and have rarely met in England but on fome family bufinefs.—Sommers Walfingham is one of the moft gay and diffipated young men about town; plays a great deal, and has eftablifhments and connections in a ftyle of expence, where I have little inclination to rival him. He was abroad when I was there laft; the French and Italians, among whom we occafionally met, were fo dazzled by the fuperior fplendour of this my magnificent coufin, that they diftinguifhed him by the title of Milor Walfingham, while I was
only

only Le Chevalier. I have often thought
it fingularly unfortunate, that the only
remaining relation i have fhould be a
man with whom I cannot be on a footing
of friendfhip, efpecially as when I die,
for I fhall now never marry, he will poffefs all my landed property, which is en-
tailed on the next male heir."

" I hope (faid Rofalie) that you will
live very long to enjoy it yourfelf, and
then tranfmit it to a family of your
own."

" There *was* (anfwered Walfingham)
a time when I thought I might be fo
happy—but that is now over !—For me,
all profpect, all poffibiltiy, of happinefs
is vanifhed—never, alas! to return."——
A long and mournful paufe now enfued,
which Rofalie had no courage to break,
though fhe would fain have fpoken words
of confolation. Walfingham at laft, fpeaking lower, and in a more dejected tone,
went on———

" For every evil, but that which I have
endured, there may be a remedy—but
the

the death of what we love!——Do you
think there can be any forrow fo deep,
and fo incurable ? ''

" Yes, (anfwered Rofalie, believing that
he found a fort of melancholy relief in
this converfation), I think the eftrangement of thofe we love may be almoft as
dreadful as their death _ _ _ _ _ _ _ _ _ _.''
She could not proceed—for fhe was fenfible that fhould either of thefe calamities
affail her, fhould Montalbert have de-
ferted her, or fhould death have divided
him from her for ever, fhe fhould totally
fail in that fortitude which fhe wifhed to
recommend to her friend ; and finding
her voice refufe to continue the argument
with firmnefs, fhe was glad of the interruption now given by Claudine, who,
coming near her, faid, " Madame, Voila
la belle Dame qui m'a fi fouvent loit
depuis deux jours, et qui fait tant des
careffes a notre petit.''——Rofalie, who
had hitherto avoided the very few ftrangers
who were occafionally feen in the village,
was now fo near the perfon of whom
Claudine

Claudine fpoke, that fhe could not efcape
her. But as fhe by no means defired to
cultivate the acquaintance Claudine had
thus begun, fhe haftily paffed on, while
the lady ftopt the Frenchwoman, to whom
fhe fpoke in her own language with great
eafe and volubility. Her figure was very
fingular; fhe was not young, and her drefs
(then lefs common than now) was in that
ftyle which women affeƐt who are above
all prejudices, and look in a morning as
if they paffed their whole lives in the
ftable or the kennel; but though the habit
and half boots might be fymptoms of a
mafculine fpirit, which fome have believed
to be the fame thing as a mafculine underftanding, the pains which had evidently been taken about her face, which
was very highly coloured, might convince
the moft fuperficial obferver, that the toi-
'let of this fair Amazonian was by no means
negleƐted.

"Surely (faid Walfingham) I have often feen that lady; it is, I think, a face
familiar

familiar to me in public places; I cannot, at this moment, recollect her name."

" I hope (faid Rofalie) *I* fhall not be under the neceffity of making any acquaintance with her; do you think fhe is ftaying here?"

" Probably, (anfwered he); but you may eafily avoid her.....Nothing is more common than for people, who are, what they fancy, retired for a few weeks to fome of thefe places, to live in a conftant exercife of the moft impertinent curiofity. Oh! I believe I now recollect who that is."

" She has fometimes a friend with her, (faid Rofalie), a younger woman, and of a lefs manlike appearance; but though they live, as Claudine tells me, in the fame houfe, and the other fcorns to be a fort of companion, I obferve fhe is often fitting with a book in her hand, and frequently feems meditating or compofing."

To this Walfingham did not anfwer, and, during the reft of their walk, which

Walfingham

Walſingham ſought purpoſely to lengthen by going about the woody environs of the nobleman's houſe * in the neighbourhood, he appeared to ſink into more than his former dejection. It was now late in the month of June, and the ſun was declining in all the radiance of that delicious month ; Roſalie, to whoſe recollection it brought the evening ſky, which ſhe had ſo often, with a deſpairing heart, contemplated from Formiſcuſa, made ſome remark on the beauty of the ſcene ; to which Walſingham, looking a moment earneſtly and mournfully in her face, ſaid ſighing, yet with a kind of impatient quickneſs——

"Ah! do not talk to me of the ſplendour of the ſun—of the beauty of nature! All—all is dead to me!—I enjoy nothing- - - - - - -" then pauſing, he added, in a low and plaintive voice——

* Lord George Cavendiſh's.

"Mon

" Mon Cœur n'a plus rien fúr la terre

" Je ne peux plus aimer, je ne peux mourir

" Pune et fainte amitié, doux charme de la vie

" Je t'immolaï l'amour ; mais qu'il m'en couté

" Reads du moins le repos a mon ame fletrie

" On dit que tu fuffis pour la felicité

" Loin de me foulager, tu comble ma mifere

" Je remplis mon deftin, je fuis nés pour fouffrir,

" Mon cœur n'a plus rien fur la terre

" Je ne peux plus aimer; je ne peux mourir."

Then paufing, he repeated the laft lines
with fome little variation——

" Mon cœur n'a plus rien fur la terre

" Ah! je n'ofe plus aimer, et ne peux mourir."

Rofalie, who underftood perfectly the
force of thefe pathetic lines, could not
help being fenfibly affected. She did not
know they were a quotation * ; and was
at once furprifed and pained by the particular manner in which the two laft lines
were a fecond time fpoken. Equally unwilling and unable to make any remarks
on what fhe had heard, and Walfingham

* From the Galatie of the Chevalier de Florian.

appearing to be difinclined to converfe, they both continued filent till they reach- ed a place where one path led to the inn, and another to the habitation of Rofalie; Walfingham there wifhed her a good even- ing, and telling her he fhould be over again foon, to know if her letters were arrived, he departed.

CHAP. XXXI.

ANOTHER week paffed, and no
letters!—Rofalie, who became every hour
more uneafy, now wifhed to confult Walfingham whether fhe ought not to write
again, and was even forming fchemes to
find Charles Vyvian, who might, perhaps,
be in England, in which cafe her friend
could greatly have affifted her, but Walfingham appeared not. In the mean time,
in her walks, Rofalie continually met the
lady who had made an acquaintance with
her little boy, and, who often courtefying
to her as they paffed, engaged her almoft
unavoidably to return the civility. Her
abode, indeed, was no longer fo retired as
it had been.

In proportion as the fummer advanced,
feveral families, who fhunned the more

gay

gay and populous bathing places, arrived; and though none of them, except the lady in queftion, appeared at all difpofed to make any acquaintance, Rofalie, who fancied herfelf the objeƈt of curiofity, was compelled.to feek walks, more diftant from the village, among the fields that arofe behind it, or on a part of the fands farther from the general refort.

Every hour of her life was now embittered by increafing anxiety; for another, another, and another day paffed without the anfwer fhe expeƈted from Mrs. Leffington. At length fhe received, to her utter difmay and confufion, 'the letters fhe had herfelf written. That to Mrs. Leffington had been opened at the poft-office, and was now fealed with the office feal, while on the cover was written——— *" No fuch perfon at Hampftead;" and again, " Left Hampftead, no direƈtion to be got whither gone."——The enclofure to Mrs. Vyvian was unopened.

The confternation and diftrefs of Rofalie were now extreme,. nor did fhe know
what

what fteps to take. After fo many days
of anxious fufpenfe, fhe was farther than
ever removed from the hopes of procur-
ing that protection which fhe felt to be
every day more neceffary; farther than
ever removed from accefs to the only
channel by which fhe might hope for intelligence of Montalbert, fhe now re-
pented that fhe had felt fo much reluctance to fee or write to Mr. and Mrs.
Blagham in her way from Portfmouth,
and that fhe had not written, on her firft
arrival, to her other (fome time) fifter,
Mrs. Grierfon, either of whom could
have informed her of Mrs. Leffington's
having left Hampftead; a circumftance
which had never occurred to her as poffible, becaufe not very probable.

To repair as immediately as fhe could
an error, which fhe now fufpected had
arifen from falfe pride and falfe fhame,
fhe thought, although late, of making thefe
applications; but having been fo much
accuftomed to rely on the opinion of
Walfingham, fhe hefitated whether fhe

ought.

ought to take any meafure without his
participation. So many days had elapfed
without his coming, that fhe thought he
was, perhaps, gone to London, or had
other engagements, and that his return
might be uncertain. Indeed were he to
be confulted, it would be impoffible for
him to give his opinion, fince he neither
knew the fingular fituation Rofalie was
in as to her real mother, or the characters
of the perfons to whom fhe thought of
applying. She recollected them, at leaft
thofe of Blagham and his affociates, with
pain. If they appeared difgufting to her,
when fhe had hardly been in focieties of
more elegance, they were likely to appear infupportable now that fhe had been
accuftomed to the intelligence and po-
lifhed manners of Montalbert and Walfingham, to whom might be added Alozzi
and De Montagny, who were men of
fafhion in their refpective countries. But
this contraft was not all that was likely
to make Blagham appear difgufting to
her; fhe dreaded his coarfe raillery on
her

her sudden departure from England, which she knew had been told in a manner very different from the truth, while the events she had to relate, as leading to her present circumstances, were so uncommon, and so little within the comprehension of people whose ideas had never travelled ten miles from their own homes, that she imagined she should inevitably expose herself to vulgar ridicule and malignant censure. The absence of Montalbert, and the presence of Walsingham, might be equally injurious to her reputation.

To the lingering suspense, therefore, in which she must remain, unless she adopted this expedient, any thing was preferable, and she determined to wait no more than one day, in which, if Walsingham did not appear, she would write to Mrs. Grierson and Mrs. Blagham, at the same time, and nearly in the same terms, that she might offend neither. The day passed, and Walsingham neither came nor sent. That evening, therefore, she sat down in a very dejected state of mind to compose

these

thefe letters. Rofalie wrote with great eafe and correctnefs; but, though what fhe now wifhed to exprefs required but few words, fhe never undertook a tafk which fhe found more difficult to perform.

To addrefs two perfons as her " dear fifters," who, fhe knew, were not related to her, was extremely irkfome; that title, when they lived together under the fame roof, and were called the children of the fame parents, had obtained for her but little of their affection, and now, that fhe had been long eftranged from them, fhe was afraid it would not procure her common civility. If fhe was confidered by them as returning in an equivocal fituation, they might repulfe her as likely to need pecuniary affiftance; if, on the contrary, fhe reprefented herfelf as the wife of Montalbert, a man whofe fortune and rank in life was fo much fuperior to thofe of the men they had married, fhe was fure of exciting their envy and indignation.——— It was better, however, to be envied than pitied, and, knowing herfelf to be Montalbert's

talbert's wife, fhe could not determine to
appear in any other light, repenting that
fhe had ever called herfelf by another
name, for which fhe now thought her
reafons were not fufficiently ftrong, and
had been too haftily adopted.

At length fhe finifhed her two letters;
in each of which fhe briefly ftated her
being returned to England without her
hufband, a circumftance which had arifen
from events too tedious to relate; and fhe
concluded with requefting to know where
Mrs. Leffington was to be heard of, and
whether her brother William, (the eldeft
Leffington, to whom fhe gave that name
without relu&tance), was ftill at Oxford.
The uncertainty of this, as he was in ex-
pe&tation of a college living when fhe
left England, was the only reafon why fhe
did not firft apply to him.

Amid the extreme difquiet, which Rofalie was in about her mother, fhe could
not but feel wonder and uneafinefs at the
long abfence of Walfingham, who had
now been more than a week without fee-

ing

ing her. The recollection of the melancholy state of mind, in which he last parted from her, added to her concern ; for
she fancied he might be ill, and she was
too sure he was unhappy. Yet she saw
the impropriety of communicating these
fears to him, or even of expressing impatience at his not coming, when he
might, perhaps, have other engagements ;
she knew, therefore, that she ought to
wait, without impatience, his promised
visit.

The little Montalbert was now between
six and seven months old, and, from his
strength and size, appeared to be more.
Claudine was extremely fond and very
careful of him, and was often entrusted
with the care of him during a short walk,
while Rosalie, who dreaded the observations that she found were made upon her,
confined herself more to the house.

Claudine, who was a lively Provinçale,
was by no means so averse to society ;
and, though her mistress always directed
her to go with the child into the most
unfrequented

unfrequented walks, fhe generally con-
trived to find fome admirable reafon for
chufing that where fhe was fure to meet
" Des beaux Meffieurs tres poli, ou
quelques dames bien honnête; qui par-
loient un peu le Francois, et qui avoient
tant, mais tant de bontis, pour elle, et tant
de joli chofes, a dire a fon petit bon
homme que c'etoit une charme."

Rofalie knew that her maid could tell
nothing of her real fituation; becaufe fhe
was ignorant of it, but fhe feared infinitely
more what fhe might imagine, though the
girl was always told that Mr. Walfingham
was only a friend, who had taken care of
her to England ; and, though fhe had
never feen any circumftance in his behaviour to contradict fuch an idea, yet
Rofalie fancied fhe had, more than once,
marked a fort of arch incredulity in the
features of Claudine : but as fhe could
not fet about affuring her he was a mere
friend, becaufe that would rather confirm
than avert fufpicion, fhe contented herfelf

G 6   with

with forbidding her to anſwer any queſ-
tions that might be made by ſtrangers,
doubting, however, whether ſhe would
obey the injunction.

Roſalie, who ſaw new faces arrive at
the place every day, occaſionally formed
wiſhes for a reſidence more ſecluded.—
Yet when ſhe conſidered that as ſoon as
ſhe could obtain intelligence of her mother, ſhe ſhould probably remove nearer
to her; and when ſhe adverted to the
convenience of being in the houſe with
very civil and quiet people, ſhe thought
herſelf hardly authoriſed to propoſe a
change. She ſhould undoubtedly have
an anſwer very ſoon from one, or both
her ſiſters, which might put an end, at
leaſt in a great meaſure, to her preſent
uncertainty.

Three days, however, paſſed before ſhe
found at the poſt-office the following
letter——

" Dear

" DEAR MADAM,.

" THEY fay that wondering makes one grow old, fo my Kate and I will not wonder, but muft confefs ourfelves a little furprifed at hearing you were fo near us,, and had ftolen a march upon us, when we thought you were among your Signors and Signoras, Italianos, and people quite out of our line ; and my Kate is not fo ready in the writing way as fome ladies, (which I don't reckon among her faults I promife you), fo you'l excufe my replying to yours of 2d inft.—To be fure you muft have dropped from the clouds, and have been quite in terra incognita, not to know that our good mother has quitted Hampftead thefe five or fix months. I fettled he raffairs there for her when I went up on the matter of Poulcat verfus Perriwinkle laft Hilary ; and fhe went to live with her fon Francis, who, you know, was always a fort of favourite ; but there was a rumpus at the houfe of Crab and

Widget

Widgett, and he quitted and fettled with his new-married wife at Carlifle. Sir Francis*, when the King pleafes, has picked up a pretty fortune I affure you, and is better off than our Epifcopus, who has alfo married a wife, and fo loft his fellowfhip ; but he's got a living, though a fmall one, and I dare fay will have a houfe full of fons and daughters. As to our olive branches, they flourifh and increafe, and my Kate has no chance of feeing much of the world this year, as we expeft a third before its end; but as I muft be at Grinftead, in a few days, for the fummer affize, where I'ye three capital caufes, I'll juft peep upon you in my way. As to the Vyvians, you know, they are grand folks, much above our cut, fo that we know nothing of them more than what every body knows. I heard that there *was* treaties going forward for the

* By thefe names Mr. Blagham diftinguifhed the two fons of Mr. Leffington.

fale

fale of Holmwood, but the entail made
by *old* Montalbert could not be dock'd
till the heir is of age ; and they fay he's
not over and above willing to accommo-
date Papa and Mama : but more of this
when we meet.—I am fomewhat at a non
plus how to direct, as my Kitty and I
wonder why you fhould have an alias to
your name ; but I fuppofe you have good
reafons.

I am, dear Madam,
Your humble fervant,
JASPER BLAGHAM.
Chichefter,
July 4, 1784."

The other letter ran thus :———

" MADAM,

" YOUR's we received.—My wife
not being very well, this ferves to inform you that Mrs. Leffington is at Carlifle, at Mr. Frank's, who is gone to live
there, and fhe with him. I do not know
that any other direction is required. My
wife

wife heard from her about six weeks ago; she was then in good health : wishing the same to you, with my wife's love and service,

I am, Madam,

Your very humble servant,

DANIEL GRIERSON.

Brockhurst Upton Farm,
    July 4, 1784;"

Though Rosalie had no reason to expect any other kind of letters than these from her two brothers-in-law, or rather those whom she had supposed such, her heart, naturally tender and affectionate, sunk in chill despondence when she reflected on the little regard there seemed to exist for her, among persons who had been accustomed to consider her as of their own blood ; and who, she believed, had never been undeceived.—" Surely, (said she), had one of them been cast alone and unprotected into my neighbourhood, I should not have hesitated a moment in

flying

flying to their affiftance."——Alas! had
fhe known more of the world, fhe would
have found this conduct of her supposed
family too common to excite a moment's
wonder; fhe would have feen that the
man of law defired to reconnoitre her
fituation before he ventured even to profefs kindnefs, left he fhould find her in
circumftances that might make fuch kindnefs expenfive; while the gentleman farmer
had no inclination to invite to his houfe
a relation of his wife's, who was either
humbled enough to give them fome trouble, or in a ftyle of life to mortify his
wife by fuperior elegance, and give her
occafion to make comparifons which might
render her, who had been reckoned a
great beauty, difcontented with the inferior lot fhe had chofen. The coldnefs,
however, of thefe letters, gave her only
momentary pain; but fhe reflected with
longer and more acute uneafinefs, that
the intelligence fhe had gained was not
only unfatisfactory, but fuch as baffled the
hopes.

hopes she had entertained of being under the protection of Mrs. Vyvian. She now was almost determined to write immediately to her mother, but the caution she had received, and the dread left her youngest daughter might be at the house, made her hesitate. It was possible too that Mrs. Vyvian might be removed from Hampstead, and to either of Mr. Vyvian's houses it was impossible for her to direct. One sentence in Blagham's letter was at once puzzling and alarming. It seemed to intimate not only a design on the part of Vyvian to sell Holmwood, which she thought would give infinite pain to his wife, but it intimated a dissention between the mother and the son, which appeared to Rosalie quite incomprehensible.

All, however, that could now be done, was to write to Mrs. Lessington; but she knew it must be at least ten days before she could have an answer. Almost worn out by the cruel suspense she had

had so long been in, and feeling every
hour an increasing distress about Montalbert, she looked forward with sensations of the deepest despondence, even
to such an interval of solicitude and
anxiety.

CHAP.

THREE of thefe fad days were paffed without any change in the fituation of Rofalie; early on the morning of the fourth Walfingham appeared.

The moment he approached her fhe was ftruck with the expreffion of his countenance, where defpair rather than dejection was marked; and, as intelligence relative to Montalbert was ever prefent to her mind, fhe was ftruck with the idea that Walfingham had learned, and was come to communicate, fome evil that had befallen her hufband. Without giving herfelf time to confider the probability of this, fhe advanced haftily towards him, and, with extreme emotion, inquired what fad tidings he brought her?——Walfing-

ham,

ham, who perhaps rather expected a gentle reproach, for his long absence, than this sudden interrogatory, answered, dejectedly and somewhat coldly—" What have I to tell you, my dear Madam?—Alas! I have nothing *new* to tell you!"

Rosalie, checked and hurt by his manner and his answer, and not able immediately to recover herself from the emotion which she had felt, could only say faintly, " I beg your pardon; I thought—I fancied—I am so unhappy, (added she), that every thing alarms me."

She sat down, and Walsingham, moved by the sight of her distress, advanced towards her, and said, " If I had learnt any good news, my amiable friend, I should not have been absent so long, for I should have been eager to have communicated whatever might give you pleasure; if bad news that related to you, so unwilling am I to give you pain, that I fear, *at this time,* my spirits would shrink from so cruel, though, perhaps, so necessary an exertion of friendship."

" Have

" Have you *yourself* any new caufe of
uneafinefs? (inquired Rofalie in a low and
faltering voice)—I hope not! "

" Ah! Mrs. Montalbert, (replied Walfingham), does there then need any new
caufe?—Does, indeed, my unhappinefs
admit of addition?"

Rofalie, ftill doubting whether fome
calamity was not known to Walfingham
which he had not the courage to tell her,
related, in a few words, the circumftances
that occurred fince they laft met ; of her
having the letter returned that fhe had
fent to Mrs. Leffington, and the unfatif-
factory anfwers fhe had received from
Mr. Blagham and Mr. Grierfon.—Walfingham read the two letters, and then
faid, " But what, my dear Madam, could
you expect from thefe fort of people—
I am forry you applied to them."—Then
thinking that he had fpoken too contemp-
tuoufly of Rofalie's relations, he added,
" I only mean to fay, that, from the
flight fketches you have give me of thefe
gentlemen

gentlemen in our defultory converfations on your affairs, it appears as if they were of an order of beings fo different from her to whom I have the honour to fpeak, that nothing more than common civility could be expe&ed of them."

" Their letters, I think, (faid Rofalie, forcing a fmile), hardly amount to that; but perceiving I had only to repair, as expeditioufly as I could, the delay that has arifen, I have written to Mrs. Lef-fington according to the direftion I ob-tained."

Walfingham then turned the converfation on indifferent fubjeƈts; but his thoughts appeared to be diftrafted, and his heart heavy. The morning was well calculated for exercife, for the fun, which was at that feafon too powerful at an early hour, was obfcured by clouds, though without any immediate appearance of rain or ftorm—Rofalie, therefore, propofed to Walfing-ham a walk on the Downs, flattering her-felf that the gloom on his fpirits might be diffipated by the pleafure he ufually took

in

in pointing out, with a degree of enthu-
fiafm peculiar to himfelf, the various appearances of the fea, or the changing
fhadows of the landfcape. Walfingham
of courfe declared himfelf ready to wait
on her, and they were juft leaving the
houfe, followed as ufual by Claudine,
when a fmug pert figure came up to them,
who looked as if he took great pains to
appear like a gentleman, with very little
fuccefs. To Walfingham he was unknown; but Rofalie immediately recog-
nifed Mr. Blagham, who, not at all abafh-
ed by feeing a ftranger with her, pranced
up to her, exclaiming, " Ah! my fweet
fifter-in-law, I have met you then at laft!
Long-parted friends, you know, (continued he, familiarly faluting her)—with
this gentleman's leave, who, I fuppofe,
is your fpoufe."—Rofalie, covered with
blufhes, anfwered coldly, " No, Sir—
that is *not* Mr. Montalbert;" and then
afking after Mrs. Blagham, fhe invited him
in, though heartily wifhing that he might
not accept the invitation.

" But

" But you were going to walk, (faid he)—I beg I mayn't be any hindrance. I can't ftay a moment—my head is full of bufinefs; a great number of caufes I affure you. . . . You know my way?——Vaftly anxious always—eh!——and have hardly time to turn myfelf about. Well! but you look purely, my fair Rofe!—I can't help remembering your former name, you fee: you look charmingly—ftill as killing as ever—lilies and rofes!—When fhall we fee Mr. Montalbert in England?"

" That is uncertain," replied Rofalie, who faw that, as Blagham was fpeaking, he turned his eyes inquifitively on Walfingham, with a look, as if to fay—Ah! ah! Sir, who are you?"

Walfingham, fufpecting that he might be the object of impertinent curiofity, and feeling already a decided averfion to Blagham, thought he fhould at once relieve Rofalie and himfelf by leaving her; he therefore faid, that, as fhe was engaged, he would not now detain her, but

Vol. III.   H   would

would take his walk. Rofalie did not
know, and yet dared not afk, whether fhe
fhould fee him again before he returned
to Haftings, for fhe had yet many things
to confult him upon. She faw him go
with regret, and it was not without an
effort that fhe concealed from Blagham
what fhe fuffered by this interruption.—
Forcing, however, an appearance of tran-
quillity fhe was far from feeling, and recollecting that fhe had now an opportunity of learning the particulars fhe fo
much wifhed to know in regard to the
Vyvian family, fhe affected to liften with
intereft to the long detail Mr. Blagham
gave her of his own affairs, which, he
faid, were very profperous and flourifh-
ing; " and (then adding) you don't know
all I have had to do with your poor
quondam lover, little Hughfon. . . . . . .
Egad! the poor fellow was over head
in ears—in love—and, faith, in debt too.
I had a fine time on't with Old Square-
toes his daddy, to make him down with
the needful ; but *at* laft we got it all fettled,

tled, and *I* patched up his pocket, poor rogue, though his heart was in a cruel plight for a long time!"

" If he had had no other grievances, (faid Rofalie), I think your friendfhip would have been put to no fevere teft; but pray tell me how and where are the Vyvians; I have been fo circumftanced fince I have been abroad as to have had no opportunity of hearing of them."

" Why, I can give you as to thofe perfonages but little information: for fince the young lady came down to Holmwood, they have never once been there, and it feems fhe took fuch a diflike to it, that, as the family were never likely to inhabit it, the Old Magnifico was trying to fell it."

" What young lady? (afked Rofalie); I don't comprehend who you mean."

" Why, the fine lady that he married— Mifs - - - - - - - - Mifs - - - - - - - - - the Honourable Mifs - - - - - - - - - ;—Well! I have a vile memory for names. However, fhe was young enough to be his

daughter,

daughter, and belonged to a Lord's family, the lady he married."

" Who married?" cried Rofalie faintly.

" Why Old Vyvian..... He married in
lefs than half a year——faith, I think they
faid it was not above three months after
the death of his wife."

" Gracious God! (exclaimed Rofalie,
thrown quite off her guard by this fhock-
ing intelligence);——Dead!—my dear,
dear benefactrefs—my beft friend - - - - -"
Stunned, by a blow fo cruel and unexpected, fhe became extremely giddy, a
cold dew covered her face, and fhe leaned againft the fide of the window on the
feat of which fhe was fitting. Blagham,
who fancied fhe was going to faint, began to call for help, and to ring the bell.
Claudine was out with the child, Rofalie
having fent her when fhe returned herfelf
with Blagham; but Mrs. Hammond, the
landlady, and her maid appeared, and the
former, terrified at the pale countenance
of her lodger, beftirred herfelf notably
for falts, hartfhorn, and water, exclaiming,

ing, at the fame time, " Dear Madam,
how ill you are !—Pray let me fend for
fomebody.—Blefs me I wifh the gentleman was here—fhall I fend Jane to call
him ? "——" Oh !—no, no ! "—was all
Rofalie could fay ; but Jane, judging that
nothing is fo great a cordial as a friend,
and having a very high opinion of Walfingham, from the liberality fhe had ex-
perienced from him, ran away without any
farther orders, and Rofalie had not recovered from the firft fhock her fenfes
had received, before Walfingham, who
had not been far from the houfe, came
in, and, agitated as much as the half-
dead mourner before him, inquired, regardlefs of the prefence of Blagham, what
had been faid to alarm her thus ; then,
turning in evident difpleafure to Blagham, he cried, " Surely, Sir, this is very
extraordinary ! "

" I'm fure I think fo, Sir, (anfwered
the attorney, who did not half like the
looks of Walfingham) ; for I had no no-
tion that Mrs. Vyvian's death could have

affected

affected Mifs Rofe——that is Mrs. -- -- --
Mrs. Montalbert I mean, in fuch a manner, or I fhould have fpoke on't more
cautioufly ; but fome people are fo ner-
vous.—Come, dear Ma'am, cheer up :—
why have a little more philofophy—we
muft all die. . . . The poor lady, you know,
had been for a long time in a declining
way ! "

Rofalie, to whom every word was as a
dagger, now arofe, and faying fhe felt
herfelf too ill to remain below, wifhed
Blagham a good morning, and tried to
add her love to his wife, with fome other
of thefe common-place fayings, that exprefs much and mean nothing; but finding herfelf unable to articulate, fhe leaned on Mrs. Hammond's arm, and retired
to her own room.

Blagham in the mean time had his curiofity awakened, which he was determined to fatisfy. Many doubts arofe as
to the reality of Rofalie's marriage. He
found her with a gentleman, whom fhe
acknowledged not to be her hufband : he

faw

faw that he took a deep intereft in whatever concerned her.... Who was he then,
and in what fituation was this young woman?—Why be directed to in one name,
and yet acknowledge another?

Blagham now attempted to enter into
converfation with Walfingham, who, dif-
liking him too much to take the trouble
of being civil at any rate, and now half-
diftracted by his fears for Rofalie, hardly
gave himfelf the trouble to anfwer him,
but walked out of the houfe, in hopes,
that when he was gone, Blagham would
quit it alfo.

But this was ill-judged, inafmuch, as
under the pretence of inquiring after the
health of *the lady*, Blagham now obtained
an opportunity of making feveral queftions to the maid as to the gentleman—
who, he learned, came with her, took the
lodgings for her, and often vifited her;
he heard too, that his name was Walfingham, and that he was, in the fimple phrafe
of Jane, " A vaftly rich gentleman, quite
as rich as a nobleman, and prodigious fond

both

both of Madam and little Mafter, though he wa'nt no near relation, only a coufin, or the like of that - - - - -."

Jane would have told more had fhe known it, but her intelligence went no farther beyond this, than that " Madam came from foreign parts ;" for Waters, who was both fenfible and faithful, had adhered punctilioufly to his mafter's ftrict injunctions, and had never mentioned more of him than his name and his fortune.

Blagham, however, had gathered much for malignant conjecture, and, as the people, with whom he was travelling to Eaft Grinftead, were by this time ready for their early dinner, he now quitted the lodgings of Rofalie, leaving his compliments and a meffage, that he hoped to hear fhe was better.

Poor Walfingham was in the mean time walking up and down a little fheltered lane near the houfe. He had never till this happened been fo fuddenly alarmed for Rofalie, and he now felt the full and painful.conviction how much his affection

for

for her had exceeded the bounds he had
at firſt preſcribed, and thought he ſhould
ever have preſcribed to it in his boſom.
The death of Mrs. Vyvian, on whom
alone, he knew, ſhe relied for protection,
though he knew not all the claims ſhe
had to it, ſeemed to have thrown her more
than ever into his power, and made her
more than before the object of his ſoli-
citude and friendſhip; and he was ſhock-
ed at being compelled to acknowledge to
himſelf, that this friendſhip was no longer
diſintereſted. He had long been conſcious, that, while he talked of his eternal
attachment to the memory of another woman, he could have found conſolation for
every loſs, if Roſalie had lived only for
him; and this conſciouſneſs was the true
reaſon why, he had abſented himſelf ſo
long, in the hope that he might, by degrees, wean himſelf from the indulgence
of a paſſion, which, if Montalbert ſtill
lived, was at once diſhonourable and deſperate. The ill ſucceſs of this experiment had given him that look of melan-

choly,

choly, and of unufual depreffion, which
had fo much alarmed Rofalie when fhe
firft faw him in the morning.

Walfingham, from a rifing ground,
where he was not himfelf perceived,
marked the departure of Blagham, and
returned to the houfe.

Rofalie had, on the fight of her child,
been relieved by a flood of tears, and
her oppreffed heart now fought ftill farther eafe in the confoling voice of a friend,
himfelf acquainted with forrow: every
prudifh fcruple vanifhed from the real
diftrefs of her mind; fhe wanted fomebody to whom fhe might talk of her loft
benefaƈtrefs, and whofe fympathy would
footh her ftill burfting heart.

Inftead, however, of hearing from him
fuch fentences of confolation as are ufually adminiftered, inftead of being advifed to have fortitude and patience, and
recommended to fubmit to inevitable
evils, Walfingham fat down and wept
with her, and, without trying to check a
fenfibility, which moft men would have
blufhed

blufhed at as a weaknefs, he feemed to
feize the opportunity of deploring anew
his own misfortunes; though unconfcious
that Rofalie lamented the death of a mother, he thought the lofs of the friend of
her early youth was a calamity great
enough to juftify the forrow fhe expreffed.
Violent paroxyfms of grief are feldom
mitigated by common-place arguments.
Walfingham therefore acted, perhaps, more
kindly, in yielding to, rather than in re-
fifting, the firft expreffions of agonifing
forrow. They fubfided, and, though the
tears ftole flowly down her cheeks as fhe
fpoke, yet Rofalie was fufficiently compofed to confult with Walfingham on the
fteps fhe had to take.

No poffible channel of hearing from
Montalbert occurred to her; fhe knew not
whither to addrefs herfelf to Charles Vyvian, or whether he was in England; and
if the Abbé Hayward yet lived, he was
alfo out of her reach: the changes that
had taken place in the Vyvian family,
fince the new connection formed by its

mafter,

master, had probably difmiffed all the old
fervants from Holmwood. Thither, however, Walfingham offered either to go
himfelf, or fend his fervant; as nothing
better occurred to him than to attempt
gaining fome intelligence of young Vyvian,
while Rofalie, who ftill thought Mrs.
Leffington her only fure means of information, determined to wait an anfwer
to the letter, which, when fhe was able to
write, he advifed her fending to Carlifle.

A filent and melancholy dinner, to
which Walfingham ftaid without being invited, was foon over. He then afked
Rofalie if air would not relieve the op-
preffion, of which, though fhe did not
complain of, it was eafy to fee hung over
her.—" If you wifh to be alone, (faid he),
I will go; but, if you will fuffer me to
walk with you, I will not intrude on your
forrows—I refpect them too much."

" I believe (anfwered Rofalie) I fhould
be better in the air; but I dread meeting
any one—indeed I am quite unfit to be
feen!"

" You

" You need not be feen, (faid he);
for by a path about a mile off, with which
I am well acquainted by my former ram-
bles along this coaft, we may go without
any hazardous defcent down the rock quite
to the fea beach, and from thence along
under the cliff called Beachy Head, where
I think you may be affured we fhall meet
no one."——Rofalie faintly objected to
this; for, as fhe never went out unat-
tended by Claudine carrying the child,
fhe thought the walk might, in his account, be rugged and dangerous. Walfingham, however, affured her that the
path he fpoke of led down to the fhore
by a defcent of hardly ten yards, and that
not fteep; he added, with a forced and
faint fmile, " I undertake for the fafe
conduct of little Harry, and you may recollect that it is not the firft time I have
had the honour of being entrufted with your
boy."—Thefe few words brought inftantly
to the mind of Rofalie the fcene of her
departure from Formifcufa, and all her
obligations to Walfingham; his active generofity

nerosity then, his unwearied friendship
since, arose sensibly to her recollection.—
" Ah! when—(thought she)—when will
Montalbert arrive to acknowledge our
weight of obligation, and to repay as much
as gratitude and attachment can repay this
invaluable friend!....When will my hufband assist me in the task I cannot execute alone, of soothing his incurable sor-
rows!—when indeed!——Montalbert!—
where are you?——what has happened to
you?——why seek you not the unfortunate Rosalie?——She is now, alas! deprived of all succour but that of a stranger.
......Oh! come then—console with her
the generous friend she has found——
mourn with her the mother she has lost!"

This melancholy soliloquy silently passed
without Rosalie's answering, or seeming to
attend to, what Walsingham had said,
though she slowly followed the way which
he led.

They hardly spoke during their walk,
except that Rosalie, observing the heavy
cloud that hung over the sun, now sink-

ing

ing weſtward, inquired of Walſingham, if
he did not think there would be a thunder ſtorm?—He anſwered, certainly not;
and they proceeded ſtill ſilently, for neither were diſpoſed for converſation.

About half a mile to the eaſtward of
their deſcent they reached that ſtupendous
ſea mark, the high cliff called Beachy
Head, which is ſeen half channel over, and
is the firſt land made in croſſing from the
oppoſite coaſt. On looking up towards
its ſummit, Walſingham ſeemed to be
ſtruck with ſome painful recollection;
he pauſed a moment, and ſaid, ſighing,
" Ah! how long it is ſince the ſight
of this head-land made my heart bound
with tranſport—ſince the cry of Beachy!
Beachy! by the ſailors, after a night paſſed in ſtruggling againſt faint and contrary
winds, announced the joyful appearance
of an old friend—but now all local attachments are at an end!—England is ſtill
my country, but I am more wretched, I
think, in it than ever, much more wretched than when I am wandering about."

Roſalie,

Rofalie, by a deep figh, fhewed that fhe fympathifed in his unhappinefs, and another long paufe enfued.

" In this cavern, (continued Walfing-ham, turning towards a deep excavation in the rock), Tradition fays, a folitary being, of the name of Darby, took up his abode. .... There are times when I am difpofed to try fome fuch experiment my-felf. I think I fhould enjoy the horrors of a ftorm, in a cave under Beachy Head. I can imagine the raging of the elements; the fwelling and foaming of the mountain billows dafhing on the rock; and the ifo-lated hermit patiently awaiting the furge, that fhould overwhelm him..... I could fancy, even now fancy, the fullen waves, which we actually hear breaking regularly and monotonoufly on the fhore, to be the hollow murmur of the fubfiding ftorm. The folitary man having efcaped the tem-peft, ventures forth from his cave!—he heard, amid the whirlwinds of the night, the cries of wretches driven on the in-hofpitable coaft, then he could not fave them!—

them!—but he now looks along the beach for their faid remains; he tries with his feeble hands to bury them.....He fees a drowned man, which, another wave will caft at his feet, he fteps forward---."

"In God's fake, Mr. Walfingham, (cried Rofalie fhuddering), forbear to draw fuch images of horror!"—"I will forbear, (anfwered he), if they diftrefs you, Mrs. Montalbert, but to me they prefent not images of horror.......Ah! no— at this moment I envy thofe who are dead;, I almoft wifh *I* were fo!"

Rofalie had often heard him talk in a defponding ftyle, but now there was in his manner dejeétion mixed with fomething of wildnefs, that made her tremble. Stunned as her mind was by its recent lofs, every vague idea had force to torment her, and fhe now again apprehended that Walfingham might know fomething of Montalbert, which the agitation fhe exprefſ- ed at their meeting in the morning, might have deprived him of courage to tell her; and that he was, by this unufual ftyle of converfation,

converfation, preparing her for it; but a moment's reflection ferved to diffipate this fear. Had it been neceffary to inflict another wound on her heart, it was not to a fcene fo remote as that which they were now in, that he would have led her; for he had feen in the morning how ill fhe could bear fuch intelligence as Blagham had abruptly given her.

Walfingham then was unhappy, more than ufually unhappy, and from fome caufe which did not perfonally concern Rofalie. The gratitude fhe owed him, and the friendfhip fhe felt for him, now called upon her to roufe herfelf and appear lefs depreffed, in hopes that *he* might become more calm. She tried, therefore, but evidently with effort, to fpeak on common and uninterefting fubjects. In their former converfations, Walfingham had frequently given her eafy leffons on botany, which, with almoft every other fcience, he underftood, fhe now, with a view to detach his mind from the fubjects that fo painfully engaged it, gathered a branch of the fea

poppy,

poppy, and another of the eryngium, that
grew among the ftones of the beach, and
began to talk of marine plants, and of
thofe of ftruĉture more fingular which
lived under the waves; fhe remarked that
thefe inhabiting the immediate margin of
the fea, apparently formed the link between marine and terraqueous vegetables,
and was proceeding thus, when, looking
at her with an expreffion of countenance,
which faid, as plainly as if he had fpoken
it—" Ah! you would not now have found
fpirits to talk on fuch fubjeĉts, if you did
not exert thofe fpirits for me!"———he
faid———

" I am a miferable being to-night, and
fit for nothing that belongs to fcience, or
perhaps to reafon. But as there are cold
unfeeling mortals, who fay, and perhaps
truly, that poetry has nothing to do with
either, I may poffibly be the better difpofed to read to you what I once wrote,
not many miles from this part of the coaft
of Suffex. It was foon after my return
from the continent, when I thought all
my

my fondeſt hopes of happineſs would be
realiſed, but when I found them vaniſhed
from my graſp for ever!—a friend, who
loved me, would not ſuffer me to remain
brooding over my ſorrows, at a houſe
I had taken, (ah! how fruitleſsly taken),
in London; but though it was late in the
year, not far, indeed, from mid-winter,
he was going to paſs a month at Brighthelmſtone, and he took me with him, care-
leſs of whither I went, and only deſiring
not to be moleſted by condolence or inquiries. . . . . . . For ſome time (continued
Walſingham ſighing) the vigilant kindneſs
of my friend would hardly ſuffer me out
of his ſight. At length convinced that
I had courage to live, he allowed me to do
as I would, and the uſe I made of my
liberty was to wander of a night along
the beach, or on the cliffs, on which
the ſea is continually encroaching. After
a long ſucceſſion of ſtormy weather, with
heavy rains, great fragments of rock fell
on the belt of ſtones beneath: the craſh
of their ſeparation and fall echoed along
the

the fhore, like thunder intermingled with
the inceffant roar of the wintry waves. . . .
My gloomy difpofition was gratified in de-
fcribing the effect of this, and thus affimu-
lating outward circumftances to my own
fad fenfations————

" The night flood *rakes* upon the ftony fhore,
   " Along the rugged cliffs, and chalky caves,
" Mourns the hoarfe Ocean, feeming to deplore
   " All that lie buried in his reftlefs waves.—
" Mined, by corrofive tides, the hollow ro..k
   " Falls prone; and, rufhing from its turfy height,
" Shakes the broad beach, with long refounding fhock
   " Loud thundering on the ear of fullen night.—
" Above the defolate and ftormy deep,
   " Gleams the wan moon by floating mifts opprefs'd,
" Yet here, while youth, and health, and labour, fleep,
   " Alone I wander;—calm untroubled reft,
' Nature's foft nurfe,' deferts the figh-fwollen breaft,
   " And flies the wretch, who only ' wakes to weep!"

CHAP.

CHAP. XXXIII.

FROM the temper of mind which Rosalie was in, the lines she had just heard Walsingham recite in a full yet mournful voice, could hardly fail of affecting her; and, while he a second time repeated them at her request, the tears slowly fell from her eyes, and it might possibly have been some time before she was enough recovered from the mournful reverie into which she had fallen, had not she and Walsingham been equally startled by the sudden appearance of two females figures from behind a projection of the cliff, on a fragment of which they had been fitting. One of them suddenly advancing to Walsingham, faid, " Upon my honour, my dear Sir, you must excuse me if I break

through

through common rules:—but I do fo doat
on talents—I am fuch an enthufiaft in
regard to poetry !——Your name is Walfingham, I think—I have often had the
happinefs of hearing of you, and once
of feeing you, at dear Mrs. Paramount's.—
I fhould be mortified—oh ! mortified beyond meafure, if I fuppofed it poffible for
you to forget it ! "

Walfingham, very little delighted with
this bold and abrupt addrefs, and recollecting at once who the lady was, determined to give her this meafurelefs mortification.—He, therefore, anfwered drily,
" That he was forry to fay his memory
refufed him the pleafure of acknowledg-
ing, as his acquaintance, à lady who did
him fo much honour."——Turning from
him with an air of pique, the admirer of
talents then addreffed herfelf to Rofalie,
and, with confidence, not at all checked
by the coldnefs of her reception, faid,
" I have been determined, my dear Madam, to make myfelf known to you ever
fince I firft faw you, and your charming
boy.

boy......What a fweet creature!—a perfect angel!——I was told when firft I faw
you, that you were an Italian lady of
rank, which only increafed my violent
inclination to be admitted among the
number of your friends; but my acquaintance, Mademoifelle Claudine, undeceived me."

Rofalie, recognizing the lady who had
fo often fpoken to Claudine, was never
fo little willing as now to make her acquaintance, and was, in truth, unable to
anfwer all thefe fine fpeeches as the laws
of common civility required; fhe, therefore, fuffered the ftranger to proceed,
only muttering fomething which her new
acquaintance deemed fufficient encourage-
ment for her to go on talking.

While this paffed, the other lady fidled
up to Walfingham, and, in the fofteft
whifper of affectation, her head reclined,
and her eyes half fhut, faid, " Is it then
indeed poffible, that Mr. Walfingham can
have fuffered the remarkable traces Lady
Llancarrick muft leave on every heart, to
be

be obliterated!—That wonderful being!
whofe talents, whofe virtues, have been
the admiration of the age in which we
live—and whofe perfon, worfhipped as it
has been and is, is the leaft of her afto-
nifhing perfections!"

Walfingham, however he abhorred every
kind of affectation, might, at another time,
have found a momentary amufement in the
fine fentimental phrafes and ridiculous
contorfions of this young woman. He recollected her to be a Mifs Gillman, whom
he had feen at parties in town, and who
had acquired the name of "*The Mufe.*"
But he was at this time fo difgufted with
her folly, and fo impatient at being thus
broke in upon, that nothing lefs than the
confideration of her being a woman, and
in inferior circumftances, (for fhe was a
humble dependent on the fcientific dames
of better fortune), could have induced
him to even the little fhew of civility
with which he anfwered—" That it was
his misfortune to have forgotten Lady

Llancarrick, owing, perhaps, to his long refidence in other countries."——" Oh! then (eagerly interrupted Mifs Gillman) you have never, perhaps, feen any of her productions.—She writes the moft divine things!—there is an originality or fublimity undefcribable in her compofitions— the effect of the ftrongeft underftanding guiding the amiable propenfities of the fofteft heart!—She did me the very high honour to defire I would walk down to this fingular fcenery, where————

" The beetling rock frowns o'er the foaming tide."

For fhe is writing fomething wherein fhe thought the wonders of nature might affift her imagination.....We were fitting penfively together my friend invoking the mufe!—and I waiting in filence the happy effufions of her fine fancy, when we were ftruck with pleafing furprife on hearing the beautiful lines you recited. They are, I am perfuaded, from your own ingenious

pen—

pen—I hope you will give them to the world."

As little more was neceffary in anfwer to this rhapfody than a bow, Walfingham now turned a forrowful look towards Rofalie, who was fuffering even a feverer penance than he had undergone, and was much lefs able to difengage herfelf.—They had rifen on the firft appearance of Lady Llancarrick and her poetical affociate, and were now walking towards home; but this did not promife to afford them the means of efcape, for the ladies declared they alfo were returning that way. Little more, however, was required during the remainder of their walk than to liften: for Lady Llancarrick having now got fomebody to hear her, to whom fhe thought all the fine things fhe had collected were entirely new, and who could not doubt of exciting wonder and admiration, was foaring into the moft elevated regions—and common life and common fenfe were left at an immeafurable diftance. She miftook the filence of Wal-

fingham

fingham (which arose from vexation and impatience) for profound ˈattention and ſilent admiration. From the firſt time of meeting him, ſhe thought him an objeɥ well worth trying to attraɥ, and wiſhed to find out the nature of his attachment to Roſalie; though, be it what it might, it impeded not her views, for it was one among her many real or affeɥed ſingularities, that ſhe pretended to have the moſt profound contempt for beauty, while her own figure and face betrayed the great pains ſhe took to acquire or preſerve in her own perſon the advantage ſhe contemned.

She knew that Walſingham was reckoned a man of the firſt underſtanding and information, and was fully perſuaded that Roſalie's youth and beauty would be weak attraɥions, when oppoſed to her charms, and thoſe talents, which alone ſhe thought had power to fix a man of his genius.

Lady Llancarrick began life as a young woman whom accidental conneɥions had raiſed into ſociety much above her fortune, and

and who thought herfelf happy to be put
on a level with them by-marrying Sir
Lodowick Llancarrick, a Welfh Baronet:
but having unfuccefsfully tried the charms
of domeftic felicity, fhe had, for fome
years, been one of thofe characters which
the undiftinguifhing multitude have called—Veteran Women of Fafhion—High
Flyers—and other appellations which are
doubtlefs quite undeferved........ The
" univerval paffion," according to Dr.
Young's defcription, was never more
ftrongly exemplified—never did a female
breaft pant fo vehemently for fame as,
that of Lady Llancarrick; and, after many
ftruggles to raife herfelf to notoriety, fhe
found every eminence pre-occupied that
might have been obtained by fingularity
of drefs or demeanour; fhe could not
drive into the temple of Fame in a Phae-
ton, four in hand, without being incom-
moded by equal or fuperior fkill—or ride
thither without being croffed and joftled;
neither could fhe leap a five-barred gate,
or do many other feats to make people

I 3   ftare,

ſtare, without having innumerable rivals.
One avenue to immortality, however, was
leſs crowded, and Lady Llancarrick followed it : ſhe became a poet and a poli-
tician—with a very moderate ſkill in her
own language, ſhe was certainly a ſin-
gular, if not a ſuccefsful, candidate for
the ʃoetic Crown; but having neither the
judgment that ariſes from natural good
ſenſe, or that which is acquired by ſtudy,
her political opinions, and her poetical
flights, were equally inconſiſtent and ab-
ſurd. Together, however, they anſwered
her purpoſe, for ſhe became *wonderful*, if
not admirable: ſome humble retainers of
the *Tuneful Nine* were always ready to
celebrate her genius; and ſhe furniſhed
ſo many paragraphs for the newſpapers,
that the editors could hardly fail of being
grateful.

But with ſo much genius could ſhe
eſcape being ſuſceptible ?—Alas !—no.—
Many inſtances were given of the ſoftneſs
of her heart, and many men of the very
firſt world had been ſuppoſed to wear her
chains.

chains. In proportion as thefe became
fragile through time, fhe had covered them
with flowers, and almoft the laft fortunate
captive, who had efcaped this charming
bondage, was Sommers Walfingham;
which, perhaps, from family partiality, infpired Lady Llancarrick with her prefent
inclination to throw the fame pleafing fet-
ters over his coufin.

Perfectly unconfcious, however, of her
defign, hardly hearing, and not at all attending to the excellent things fhe was
faying, Walfingham walked by her fide,
accufing his deftiny of cruelty in com-
pelling him to part with Rofalie for fome
time, and to leave her in fuch a ftate of
mind, without having an opportunity of
faying to her much that he had poftponed
till he took leave, and which now appeared abfolutely neceffary to his own
peace, if not for the guidance and confolation of his interefting unhappy friend.
Yet, however, he wifhed to have a long
converfation with Rofalie before he rode
back to Haftings, he was fo perfuaded

that

that Lady Llancarrrick and Mifs Gillman had forced themfelves thus into his no-tice, only to gratify impertinent curiofity, or find ground for malignant remark in regard to Rofalie, that he determined, whatever it might coft him, not to put it in their power. For a moment he thought of returning to her lodging, after they had fhaken off their unwelcome companions; but, confcious that fo unufual a vifit muft excite the invidious remarks of the woman of the houfe, and fufpecting that Lady Llancarrick and her companion would watch his fteps, he found himfelf com-pelled, on Rofalie's account, to relinquifh the idea of feeing her again that evening; but rage and vexation feized him, and he no longer wore even the femblance of ci-vility, though Lady Llancarrick did not, or would not, perceive it. Their way lay near the door of the inn where Walfing-ham's horfes were put up. His groom was walking before it waiting his orders; he called to him impatiently, and bade him bring the horfes out; they followed him

in

in an inftant, when, approaching Rofalie, he wifhed her a good night, and faid, in a low voice, that he would fee her in a very few days; then, coldly bowing to the other two ladies, he mounted his horfe, and was out of fight in a moment.

Rofalie, trying to fupprefs a figh that arofe partly from regret at his going fo fuddenly, and partly from recollection of the ftate of mind in which fhe knew he was, was now very coldly and formally courtefying her good night to her two unwifhed-for companions; but they did not intend to let her off fo eafily, and Lady Llancarrick, bidding her dear Gillman take the arm of her fweet friend, faid, " Oh! we will fee her fafe to her lodgings, you know ! "

The diftance was not far, but Rofalie thought it now lengthened on purpofe: both the ladies befetting her with queftions which fhe could not anfwer truly, and would very fain have been excufed from anfwering at all. Indeed, during the former part of their walk, while Lady

1 5.   Llan-

Llancarrick had engaged Walfingham, the gentle, fentimental Erminia Eliza Gillman had, albeit in the fweeteft accents and with the moft infinuating foftnefs, put fo many queftions to poor Rofalie, that greater art and knowledge of the world, than fhe poffeffed, would have been neceffary to prevent the fly fentimentalift from difcovering that there was a great deal of myftery in her affairs, and that their obfcurity arofe from their being of a nature which fhe dared not reveal, yet knew not how artfully to hide.

When, at length, Rofalie was once more alone in her own parlour, all the events of the day revived in painful confufion to her memory ; but the death of her mother fwallowed up every other forrow, and, with a flood of tears, fhe accufed herfelf of infenfibility, for having, at fuch a time, fuffered any other confideration to call off her thoughts a moment from that object of juft and endlefs regret. Of the two ladies fhe had feen, fhe thought no more than to determine upon not continuing

nuing their acquaintance, and rather to
quit the place than to affociate frequently
with people fo utterly difagreeable.—Her
heart heavy with regret, and her head
aching from having wept fo much during
the day, fhe drank a glafs of water and
haftened to her bed, where the moft tor-
menting reflections, on the cruel fate of
her beloved mother, long prevented her
tafting any repofe. At length wearied
nature gave her up to momentary forget-
fulnefs; but fhe had hardly flept an hour,
when fhe was awakened by one of the moft
violent ftorms of thunder, lightning,
wind, and hail, that fhe ever recollected
to have heard. For herfelf fhe was unconfcious of apprehenfion, but clafping
to her palpitating heart its only certain
poffeffion, her lovely child, fhe fhrunk
from the flafhing fires which made their
way through her window fhutters; fhe
endeavoured, however, to appeafe the fears
of Claudine, who crept into her room
half dead with terror, but fuddenly, as
fhe was reafoning with her maid, fhe re-

collected

collected that, from the time which had paffed fince Walfingham fet out, it was impoffible he could have reached Haftings. Her apprehenfions, left any evil might befal him, and the idea that fhe was the innocent caufe of his being expofed, became extremely painful to her bofom; fhe yielded to thofe gloomy thoughts which too frequently aggravate forrow—and exclaimed, " Alas! *I* am fo unfortunate, that it feems as if I communicated calamity to all who are interefted about me......Born the child of profcription, *I* deftroyed the peace of my mother, and on my account it probably was, that my unhappy father was driven into exile!—Should *he* have furvived long years of calamity, I fhall never behold him, never have an opportunity of expreffing for him the filial tendernefs I fhould feel, or of weeping with him over the memory of my dear, dear mother. Again profcribed in my marriage, I have, perhaps, undone Montalbert, and loaded him with the malediction of his mother......Perhaps—

oh!

oh! thought too terrible to be dwelt upon!——perhaps his tendernefs for me may have coft him his life, and he may have perifhed amid the fulphurous gulphs and unwholefome exhalations at Meffina. —No, I will not encourage fuch an idea. The precautions of his cruel mother coun- teraƈted it, and, by doing fo, made my imprifonment and perfecution' favours.— Alas! I have prefent evil enough with- out dwelling on the paft.—The noble- minded, the difinterefted Walfingham, feems to be infeƈted with my unhappinefs; perhaps, even now, is the viƈtim of his generous attention to me!—and you, dear little unconfcious companion of my woes, fole fweetener of my forrowful exiftence, may not you one day lament that you were ever born?"

This refleƈtion was too diftreffing— and an ardent prayer to Heaven, that *fhe* alone might fuffer, and that her boy might be as happy as fhe was miferable, ended the fad foliloquy.—The violence of the tempeft abated, but not till morning broke.

Rofalie,

Rosalie, after a short interval of rest, arose; she heard from her maid, as well as from her other servant and the people of the house, melancholy details of the mischief occasioned by the lightning; of which some particulars were true, but the greater part much exaggerated, or wholly groundless.

Rosalie, still depressed by the idea of Walsingham's possible danger, and by the effects of a sleepless night, tried to shake off both her mental and personal uneasiness by a walk. It was an hour when she hoped that she might venture to the sea side without meeting either of the ladies whom she so much desired to avoid. In this, however, she was disappointed :— they joined her as she returned home; talked over the circumstance of the storm— Lady Llancarrick declaring that she enjoyed its sublime horrors, and Miss Gillman tempering the same sentiment, with delicately expressing concern for the fate of those who might have suffered in it.

" Apropos,

" Apropos, (faid Lady Llancarrick)—
my dear Mrs. Sheffield, do you know it
came into our heads, as Gillman and I
fat together looking at the lightning over
the fea, that *our* agreeable acquaintance,
Mr. Walfingham, could hardly have reached whatever place he was going to before the tempeft came on :—he refides, I
think, at fome diftance ? "

As fhe faid this, fhe fixed on Rofalie
her fierce inquiring eyes. Rofalie, though
no human being could be more void of
offence, blufhed deeply, and, before fhe
could form a reply, Walfingham's groom
came up to her, and delivered a packet
with his mafter's compliments, and he had
orders to wait for an anfwer.

Rofalie now faw, in the countenances
of the two ladies, an expreffion which
added, for a moment, to her pain and
confufion. Relieved, however, from the
uneafinefs fhe had been in about Walfingham, fhe felt all the dignity of confcious innocence, and refolved to difregard

gard cenfure, which, whatever appearances
might fay, fhe knew herfelf incapable of
deferving; fhe recovered her compofure,
and telling the fervant fhe would return
home and write an anfwer, which he might
call for in a quarter of an hour, fhe flightly
wifhed the two ladies a good morning, and
left them.

Their curiofity, which was ftrongly excited on many accounts, they fcrupled not
to attempt gratifying by queftioning the
"fervant; from whom, however, they obtained but little additional information.
While thefe ladies were thus unworthily
employed, Rofalie read the following letter
from Walfingham————

LETTER.

" I was compelled to leave you, dear
Madam, laft night in an uneafy ftate of
mind—for how could I be otherwife,
when I faw you in fuch depreffed fpirits;
and I fear your new acquaintances are

not

not of that defcription of women, with
whom, either in the hour of fadnefs or
gaiety, you would wifh to affociate.—I
hope, that if you find them too much difpofed to trefpafs upon you, you will not
fuffer the fear of violating the common
forms of fociety to force you into the
moft uneafy of all reftraints, keeping up
a fhew of regard to conceal diflike and
difguft. I believe neither of them to be
worthy of the friendfhip of Mrs. Montalbert. You know, I hope, that if this or
any other circumftance renders your prefent abode lefs agreeable to you, my fervices fhall be exerted to find one more
eligible—but favour me with your commands immediately, as I fhall go to-morrow to London, to plead with an old
acquaintance of my father's on behalf of
an unfortunate fon, who, having two years
ago married a young woman, whofe only
fault was her being deftitute of fortune,
has been abandoned by his family, and,
having been brought up to no profeffion,

is

is in a very diftreffed fituation, with a wife
and two fweet little children.   I met him
a few days before I had laft the honour
of feeing you, as he is here with his family; I bade him confider what i could
do to ferve him, and he has defired me to
fee his father on his behalf: perfuaded
that I fhould fucceed in reftoring him to
comfort and his father.   Without having
very high ideas of my powers of perfuafion, efpecially when the hard-cold heart
of avarice is to be moved, I will, however, make the attempt, and, unlefs there
is any thing in which I can firft have the
pleafure of being employed for you, Madam, I fhall begin my journey to-morrow
early.   My friend's father lives in Not-
tinghamfhire.

" May the bearer of this bring me as
favourable an account of your health and
fpirits as can be expected after the juft
concern you have fo recently felt:—I hope
you were not terrified by the tempeft of
laft night.   It overtook me on a place

fo

fo wild and dreary, that I could have fuppofed it the fcene where Shakefpeare imagined the meeting between Macbeth and
the Weird Sifters. The fpot I allude to
is a wide down; in fome places fcattered
over with fhort furze, in others barren
even of turf, and the uncloathed chalk
prefenting the idea of cold defolation :—
on the left is a ruined chapel, or fmall
parifh church, in which fervice is per-
formed only once in fix weeks; on the
right are, in fome places, marfhes that
extend to the fea—in others a broad fpit
of fand and ftones, where nature feems to
refufe fuftenance even to the half-marine
plants, which, in moft places, are thinly
fprinkled among the faltpetre of the
beach.

"The hollow murmur of the diftant
fea, on which the lightning faintly flafhed, foretold the coming ftorm fome time
before I reached this heath—there it overtook me; but as there are times when
outward accidents make little or no impreffion on me, I quickened not my pace;
and

and fhall I own it without incurring the
charge of affeѐted eccentricity, that I
found a melancholy fpecies of pleafure
in furveying the gloomy horrors of the
fcene——in fancying I was the only human being abroad, within the circuit of
many miles—in cherifhing the fame fpirit with which Young fays in his 'Night
Thoughts——

'Throughout the vaſt globe's wide circumference.
'No being wakes but me.'

Yet I was more moderate, and more phi-
lofophical in my fombre enjoyment; and,
when I came to my lodgings, I wrote what
follows, which I beg you will put into the
fire when you have read——

"Swift fleet the billowy clouds along the ſky,
"Earth feems to ſhudder at the ſtorm aghaſt;
"While only beings, as forlorn as I,
"Court the chill horrors of the howling blaſt.
"Even round yon crumbling walls, in fearch of food,
"The ravenous owl forgoes his evening flight;
"And in his cave, within the deepeſt wood,
"The fox eludes the tempeſt of the night:—

"But,

" But, to my heart, congenial is the gloom
" Which hides me from a world I wiſh to ſhun—
" That ſcene, where ruin ſaps the moulding tomb,
" Suits with the ſadneſs of a wretch undone;
" Nor is the darkeſt ſhade, the keeneſt air,
" Black as my fate—or cold as my deſpair."

CHAP.

CHAP. XXXIV.

THE penſive, or rather gloomy diſpoſition in which Walſingham wrote, was
but too congenial to the feelings of his
unhappy correſpondent, who paſſed the
reſt of the day in her houſe, indulging
melancholy reflections. She was glad,
however, that he was gone an excurſion
likely to divert his thoughts, and knew
that nothing ſo effectually won him from
himſelf as ſuch a generous ſervice as he
was now engaged in. The following day
aroſe, and found her in the ſame dejected
ſtate of mind; left alone, without even
the expectation of ſeeing Walſingham, or
of hearing any intelligence, which, he aſſured her, he would not fail to attempt
collecting as to Montalbert, or Charles
Vyvian, ſhe had nothing to look forward

to

to but the anfwer fhe yet hoped to receive from Mrs. Leffington; and fhe reckoned daily when the courfe of the poft
might give her, at leaft, this melancholy
fatisfaction.

A mind, thus preying on itfelf, agitated
by hopes and fears, and wearied by conjectures, could only be relieved, at leaft,
for a few hours by books of amufement.
She had fent to the only library in the
place for two or three of thefe fort of
books, but finding them only pages of in-
anity, which could not a moment arreft
her attention, fhe determined, notwithftanding her fears of again meeting Lady
Llancarrick and Mifs Gillman, to go to
the fhop, and endeavour to pleafe herfelf
better. In doing fo, fhe was under the
neceffity of paffing through that part of
the village moft frequented. Congratu-
lating herfelf, however, on not having met
any body, fhe was returning, with her
books in her hand, when her former perfecutors, fuddenly advancing from their
lodgings, joined her, and, with their ufual
                                    carelefs

carelefs eafe, entered into difcourfe with
her, afking feveral queftions, and, when
to evade thefe, fhe turned the converfation on the books fhe had been in fearch
of, the elder lady delivered her opinion
of feveral celebrated and new productions,
with a fluency which aftonifhed Rofalie,
fo much did it refemble a differtation
learned by heart, and remind Rofalie of
Jenkinfon in the Vicar of Wakefield, who,
whenever he met a ftranger, began with—

" Sir, the cofmogony, or creation of
the world," &c. &c.

Rofalie, however, better content to be
a hearer than a fpeaker, liftened, or appeared to liften, with perfect refignation,
internally refolving, however, to take her
leave as foon as fhe arrived at the turning which led to her own lodgings, whether the harangue was finifhed or not;
fhe walked, in the mean time, quietly
along between the two ladies, (Mifs Gillman having taken her arm), and gazing
on the ground, as if fhe was counting the
pepples; when two perfons haftily approached,

proached, and a voice exclaimed—" It is fhe!—it is my wife!——By Heavens it is herfelf!"——The voice was Montaltalbert's—Rofalie raifed her eyes—it *was* Montalbert himfelf.

Almoft unconfcious of what fhe did, fhe fprang forward, and would have thrown herfelf into his arms, but he retired from her, with rage and refentment in his countenance, which fuddenly changing into an expreffion of pity, he cried—" Lovely, loft creature!—art thou, indeed, loft to me?——Yes—for ever loft!—and here—too well convinced that all I have heard is true—here we part for ever!"

Rofalie, who had advanced towards him, heard all this with a furprize and terror that deprived her of the power of utterance. She tried, however, to fay, " For mercy's fake, Montalbert, hear me!"—but feeing that he ftill retreated from her, and that feizing the arm of the perfon with him, he even walked haftily away; fhe made a vain attempt to quicken her pace and follow him, but her trem-

bling limbs refufed to fecond her will—
her head grew giddy, her heart ceafed for
a moment to beat, and fhe would have
fallen, had not Mifs Gillman, who, with
Lady Llancarrick, beheld this fcene with
wonder, ftepped forward and fupported
her.

In another moment fhe recovered her
fenfes, and, looking wildly round her,
exclaimed, " Where is he ?——Where is
Montalbert ?——Lead me, if you have
pity—lead me to him! .... Let me follow
him—for God's fake let me ! ''——Mifs
Gillman, with the common phrafes ufed
on fuch occafions, befought her to be
compofed ; Lady Llancarrick began to
reafon, and to prove very logically that
nobody ought to give way to fuch violent
emotions. Her eyes, however, had followed Montalbert till he difappeared ;—
though when Rofalie eagerly inquired
which way he went, it was a piece of intelligence fhe did not chufe to communicate.

Rofalie,

Rofalie, when her fenfes and recollection returned, defired to go to her lodgings, but, as it was evident fhe was incapable of walking thither without affiftance,
the two ladies of courfe attended her.——
Mifs Gillman, in the few intervals allowed
her, fpoke moft fentimentally and patheti-
cally, while the lady of fuperior talents
affected to argue on the impropriety of
yielding to extravagant expreffions of grief
or joy—not without fome hints, that fhe
could not comprehend how the gentleman they had feen could be the hufband
of Mrs. Sheffield, and yet be called Montalbert. Rofalie attended to neither of
her new friends; fhe hardly knew who
was with her; but, having formed a confufed conjecture that Montalbert might
be at her houfe, her eager eyes were inquiring for him the moment fhe came in
fight of it. Claudine met her with the
little boy; but Montalbert had not been
there. In beholding her child, he recalled to her ftartled fenfes the conduct of his
father, with his wild behaviour and ftrange

expreffions,

expreſſions, and all the agitation of her
ſpirits returned; but ſhe was relieved by
a flood of tears, and ſobbed violently—
while ſuch comfort or remonſtrance, as
the ladies thought might either conſole
or determine her to bear her diſtreſs with
fortitude, were alternately adminiſtered.—
Roſalie had nothing to anſwer. She wiſhed, though ſhe could not propoſe it, that
they would leave her as the only kindneſs
they could do her; and at length, the one
having exhauſted all her ſentiment, and
the other all her reaſoning, they went
away, promiſing to call in the evening
to ſee how ſhe did. Roſalie aſſured them
ſhe ſhould be very well, and begged they
would not trouble themſelves; ſhe affected a momentary tranquillity, to eſcape
from a repetition of attentions, which, as
they appeared to be well meant, ſhe could
not rudely refuſe.

When they were gone, the aſtoniſhed
and ſtunned mind of Roſalie returned to
a new contemplation of the ſcene that had
paſſed; when ſhe recalled the countenance.

nance, the words, and the attitude, of
Montalbert, it appeared, but too certain,
that her actions had been misreprefented,
and that jealousy and anger poffeffed him.
How could she find—how appease him?—
Whither was he gone?—He had come in
search of her; was he then so prejudiced
against her, that he would not even hear her,
that he would not even fee the child whom
he had so paffionately loved?—Thefe reflections, preffing with painful violence on
her mind, deprived her for fome time of
the calmnefs that might have enabled her
to determine what fhould be done. She
fometimes thought of going out to inquire
for Montalbert, then found herfelf unequal to the dread of meeting him, whom
fhe had fo long fought and fo tenderly
beloved, only to have her heart pierced
by founds of anger and reproach, from a
voice in which fhe had been ufed to liften
to the fondeft language of adoring love.—
She had no fervant who either knew the
perfon of Montalbert, or had fufficient
fteadinefs and fenfe to perform fo delicate

K 3

a com-

a commiffion as that which fhe wifhed to
have executed. The woman of the houfe,
though older and graver than Claudine,
was very ignorant, and to her it would be
impoffible to explain fuch a hiftory as
hers, and equally impoffible to make her
comprehend it. To her ever generous, con-
fiderate, and fenfible friend, Walfingham,
the thoughts of Rofalie naturally turned;
but had he been ftill at Haftings, fhe
could not have ventured to have afked
his mediation. It was too evident, from
the few incoherent words Montalbert had
uttered, that his unkindnefs and violence
originated in jealoufy, and of whom, be-
fides Walfingham, could he have conceived fuch injurious ideas?

Amidft thefe fluctuating thoughts one
occurred to her, which compelled her to
take fome immediate refolution. If fhe
could fee Montalbert, when fhe was lefs
under the influence of furprife, fhe thought
fhe could talk to him calmly, and fhould be
able to convince him that fhe had never,
even in idea, fwerved from the faithful
tendernefs

tendernefs fhe owed him : but to avail herfelf of this hope no time was to be loft. Montalbert might have left the village; and where was fhe then to feek him, that he might hear her juftification. Impreffed then with a conviction that fhe ought to find him inftantly, fhe was haftening to leave the houfe, when the following note was delivered to her———

" THE father of the unfortunate child, known by the name of Henry Montalbert, requires to have him immediately delivered to the two perfons who attend for that purpofe, and who will conduct him to

H. MONTALBERT."

Rofalie read this cruel order : fhe ftood for a moment like the ftatue of defpair— her blood circulated no longer; fhe was choaked by the convulfive ftruggles of her heart—but fhe could not weep, fhe could not even fpeak. The two perfons, who were fent for her child, appeared at

the

the door of the parlour into which she had returned, and, at the same moment, by another door, Claudine entered with the little boy. Rofalie ftarted up, and eagerly feizing him in her arms, uttered a few incoherent words—" They fhall not take you from me, my child, (faid fhe); let them rather kill me at once!"—Then, turning towards the man and woman, who approached without any apparent feeling for her inexpreffible diftrefs, fhe cried, her voice half ftifled by fobs, " For mercy's fake, whoever you are, lead me to Montalbert!—Do not, oh! as you hope for Heaven—do not execute his cruel order, but let me find him—I will carry my child to him myfelf!"

The man, who had a countenance which feemed made on purpofe to execute fuch commiffions, anfwered, with fullen coldnefs, " Madam, we can fay nothing to all this—we muft obey the order of our employer—we act legally, and cannot enter into any difcuffion.....Come, Mrs. Jacklin, we have no time to lofe."

So

So faying, he approached with his companion as if to take the child. Rofalie could only prefs her boy more clofely to her breaft, and, uttering a faint fhriek, funk with him upon her knees—" Have mercy!—oh! have pity upon me!"——was all fhe could utter. The unfeeling man, regardlefs of her agonies, or of the tears and fhrieks of Claudine, who wept, implored, and menaced, forced the child from the convulfive grafp of its apparently dying mother, and putting it into the arms of the woman, they haftened from the houfe.

Rofalie, who had funk upon the floor, feemed, as if by a miracle, to recover herfelf. She rofe, and, with wild looks and fwift fteps, purfued the cruel wretches who had thus torn her child from her : but they were already out of fight; her ftreaming eyes fought them in vain; her head became giddy; her fenfes forfook her, and fhe would have fallen had not Claudine caught her in her arms, and fupported her till the woman of the houfe

coming

coming to her affiftance, they carried her between them into the houfe, infenfible and apparently dead.

She was now placed on her bed, and the remedies ufual in fuch cafes were adminiftered; fhe opened her eyes, and, eagerly fixing them on the face of Claudine, inquired for her child. Claudine could anfwer only by her tears. The miferable mother then feized the hand of the woman of the houfe, conjuring her to go in fearch of him: but recollecting how little fuch a perfon could be interefted, fhe attempted to rife herfelf, and again follow him. The women refufed to fuffer her, and endeavoured to appeafe her by promifes of going themfelves; but her impatience became greater, and fhe raved, entreated, and wept, till the violence of her emotions exhaufted her, and fhe funk in total depreffion. A few moments fufficed to recover her to a fenfe of her mifery, and then the fame fad fcene was renewed.

At

At length the woman of the houfe agreed to go out on inquiry, and fomething like hope fufpended for a while the agonies Rofalie had fuffered; but when the good woman came back, and related, though in the moft cautious way fhe could, that the child had been carried away in a poft chaife by the two perfons who had fetched him from his mother—the unhappy Rofalie relapfed into all the horrors of defpair. The whole night paffed in incoherent ravings, in calling wildly for her child, or imploring the mercy of its father, while Claudine ftood weeping on one fide of the bed, and the landlady remonftrating and praying on the other. Before morning her fenfes feemed to have forfaken the wretched fufferer: yet her ftrength was fo little impaired, that fhe again infifted on being fuffered to follow her child. She directed Claudine to get her a poft chaife; then attempted to rife and drefs herfelf, till, giddy and fick, fhe funk again on the bed. Thither the woman of the houfe had by this time fummoned an apo-

thecary,

thecary, who began gravely to inquire into the caufe of the agitation in which he faw his patient. Claudine could not explain it, and the good woman knew not how, fo that, from what fhe faid, the apothecary, concluding fhe had loft a child by death, commenced a grave harangue on fubmiffion and acquiefcence, which ferved only to add to the tortures of the unfortunate young woman: nor was this gentleman, who really meant well, her only tormenter. Her landlady had fent for Lady Llancarrick and Mifs Gillman, who, taking each their ftation on the oppofite fides of her bed, began to adminifter confolation, fuch as is ufually doled forth in fet phrafes, with fome difference, however, arifing from character ; for the lady fpoke like a philofopher ; *" the Mufe"* like a fentimentalift— while Rofalie, unable to anfwer either, repeated to herfelf in the anguifh of her heart————

" She talks to me who never had a fon." So totally unqualified were all thefe parties for the delicate office of comforting

the

the afflicted, or so unfit was the mind of
Rosalie for receiving consolation, that,
before evening, her spirits were agitated
to a fearful degree; her reason was evidently wavering; and, no longer conscious of the inutility of her exclamations,
she called incessantly for her child; then
implored her husband to pity her; and
from thence her thoughts made a sudden
transition to the scenes she had passed,
through in Sicily and at Formiscusa; till,
at length, all she said appeared so incoherent, and was so little understood by
those who heard her, that they became
convinced her senses were totally deranged,
and, that these wild and incoherent appeals
to persons, as well as her descriptive ravings about places, were the effects of a
disordered imagination.

Lady Llancarrick, who was writing for
the stage, contemplated this sad spectacle
with the sang froid of an amateur, who
hoped to add some strong touches to her
performance; while her more gentle friend,
with her attempts at shewing sensibility,

was

was confidering how fuch an incident might weave into a novel ; but neither felt any true fympathy for the unhappy object, who, in the early bloom of youth, was thus the prey of anguifh, which was reducing her to infanity or death.

The woman of the houfe, however, and the apothecary of the village, began, after the third and fourth day, to be ferioufly alarmed for the unfortunate patient, inftead of recovering her recollection, continued to fluctuate between violent ravings and fits of gloomy ftupidity, while an alarming fever continually preyed upon her.— The ladies, who had at firft appeared to attend her with patience and humanity, now flackened in their good offices: Lady Llancarrick found that neither Walfingham nor Montalbert appeared; that fhe had no chance of making an interefting or profitable acquaintance by her affected humanity, and that fhe might, perhaps, be involved in trouble, and even in expence; to both of which, but particularly the latter, fhe had a decided averfion. As to

Mifs

Mifs Gillman, fhe had no will of her own, but contented herfelf with gentle repetitions of the words, " Poor dear creature!—Sweet unfortunate!——alas! how pitiable!"——While fhe occafionally addrefled to her patronefs eulogiums on her benevolence.—" How good your ladyfhip is!—oh! what a heart, my dear friend, is yours!—what amiable fympathy for the diftreffed!"——Thefe fentences were continually fighed forth from the delicate fenfibilities of the fentimental Mufe, and received by the lady as if fhe had really deferved them.

Ah! little could the confolations of fuch people avail towards healing the wounds of a broken heart. The unfortunate Rofalie every day became worfe and worfe. Claudine could not aft for her; a ftranger herfelf, and naturally helplefs, fhe could only fit and weep by the bedfide of her expiring miftrefs; or, when fhe appeared to have an interval of fenfe, afk directions of her, which Rofalie was unable to give,

or

or which, if given, were incoherent and impra&icable.

The apothecary now confulted Lady Llancarrick on the propriety of fending for a phyfician. Uncertain how far the finances of the fufferer might anfwer fuch an expence, and fearful of being called upon herfelf to fupply any deficiency, Lady Llancarrick would give no advice; the landlady doubted how far enough remained, in cafe her lodger died, to difcharge the arrears that would be aue, and to pay the expences which might be incurred; while Claudine, who had not the fmalleft idea of the mercenary principles on which thefe people acted, was continually imploring Lady Llancarrick to fend for other advice, till, from this fort of importunity, fhe gradually withdrew; while Mifs Gillman gravely held forth an opinion, that, perhaps, after all, this pretty young creature, for whom they had been interefting themfelves, and whofe adventures appeared to have fomething fo extraordinary

traordinary in them, might be merely a girl in inferior life, to whom fome man of fafhion had attached himfelf, and, finding her unworthy of any long or ferious partiality, had taken his child from her for very proper reafons. While thefe two good ladies were thus prudently fettling that they ought to decline any farther interference, the illnefs of the wretched Rofalie increafed to fuch a degree, that the apothecary believed, and her female attendants were convinced, fhe had not many hours to live.

CHAP.

CHAP. XXXV.

FIVE days had now paffed, five melancholy days, fince the fad victim of unjuft fufpicion had found no relief from anguifh, but in her moments of infenfibility. Her lovely face was quite faded and changed; her form emaciated and enfeebled, fo that fhe could hardly fupport herfelf in her bed; fometimes fhe wildly ftarted up, looked round her, and inquired for her child, until fome degree of recollection funk her again into the torpor of defpair.

It was on the evening of the laft of thefe days that three gentlemen, attended by fervants, ftopped in a poft coach at the door of the houfe, and inquired for Mrs. Montalbert. The landlady, who hoped that their arrival would put an end

to

to her apprehensions of pecuniary loss, eagerly assured them that the lady was there; she was very ill to be sure—" But I will call Mam'selle, her maid, (added the good woman); and, for certain, Madam, will be glad to see her friends."

The three strangers, on this information, left their coach, and entered the parlour. One of them appeared to suffer from ill health; he was pale and sallow, and, though yet in the middle of life, seemed to have been the victim of sorrow or disease. The second had the habit and air of a clergyman; and the last was a young man, apparently of fashion, who might have been taken for the son of the one, and the pupil of the other.

Claudine, who, amidst all her solicitude for her mistress, never lost sight of a little personal vanity, staid to adjust her cap at the glass, to put a little powder in her hair, and a nicer fichu on her shoulders; and then expecting certainly to see Mr. Walsingham, whom she considered, in some measure, as her master, she fluttered down

down into the room, where, in his place, she beheld three gentlemen who were entirely strangers to her.

The elder of them began to question her on the situation of her lady; but finding she understood little English, the younger, who spoke like a native of France, took up the inquiry, and heard, with great apparent concern, the sad account of Rosalie's health, which even the warmth and earnestness of Claudine's manner could but little exaggerate. Each of her auditors seemed almost equally affected, and each inquired whether she could conduct them to her mistress. Claudine, not knowing what to do, and having no idea of who these people could ·be, answered, in visible alarm, that she would go and inquire; forgetting, at that moment, that her poor mistress was probably incapable of attending to any question she might put to her, and certainly incapable of conversing with strangers.

It was in vain she spoke to Rosalie; she attended not to her. At length Claudine

dine thought of a ftratagem fhe had before ufed with fome fuccefs, when it was
neceffary to roufe her unhappy miftrefs
to temporary exertion—fhe fpoke of her
child; and Rofalie, who had appeared
totally infenfible for fome moments, raifed
her languid head on her arm, and fixing
her dim eyes on Claudine, faintly bad her
repeat what fhe had been faying.

Claudine then told her, that three gentlemen were below, who, fhe was fure,
were her friends, and who certainly came
to tell her fome good news about the
dear little boy. Rofalie, catching eagerly
at the hope thefe words offered, feemed
to make an effort to recal her diffipated
and confufed fenfes to a point worthy her
attention. Claudine faw that fhe had gained her notice, and repeated all fhe had faid,
enforcing, with her utmoft power, the idea
that the three gentlemen in queftion were
certainly fent by Montalbert to treat of
a reconciliation, and reftore her child.

Rofalie by degrees acquired fo much
power over her fcattered and enfeebled
spirits,

fpirits, as to attempt recollecting what
friends were moft likely to be charged
with fuch a commiffion; but her intellects
were not equal to the refearch; bewildered and confufed, fhe put her hand to her
head, and fighing deeply, fhe appeared to
give up the inquiry in defpair. There
were no friends of hers who anfwered
the minute defcription Claudine had given
of the ftrangers; nor did fhe know of
any friends of Montalbert's, who were
either acquainted with his marriage, or
likely to be in his confidenece. Hope,
however, enabled her to re-affume her
powers of reflection, and fhe became
confcious, that, whoever the perfons might
be who thus interefted themfelves in her
affairs, fhe ought to fee them, if they
were Montalbert's friends, on his account; if they were her friends, on their
own.

But when it was neceffary to make the
exertion, which her returning reafon told
her was neceffary, her ftrength fo failed
her, that it was more than an hour before

fore fhe was feated, by the affiftance of the landlady, in an arm chair, and half an hour longer before fhe had, by the aid of hartfhorn and water, obtained refolution enough to let Claudine go down with a meffage, that any one of the gentlemen who were moft difpofed to take the trouble of vifiting a fick room, was defired to walk up.

An interval of fome moments paffed before a foot was heard on the ftairs; but Rofalie, fo far from finding her courage ftrengthened by the delay, had become almoft fenfelefs and breathlefs, when the door was opened by Claudine, and the figure which appeared at it fhe juft diftinguifhed to be Charles Vyvian, before her fight and confcioufnefs totally forfook her, and fhe fell back in the chair, towards which he eagerly flew to fupport her.

" My fifter! (cried he)—my dear, dear Rofalie!—But is it, indeed, my Rofalie!—Good God! how changed!—how altered!——Where is Montalbert?—what has

has happened?—and why are you reduced to this fituation ? "

Rofalie heard him not ; but Claudine, amidſt her efforts to recover her miſtreſs, related all ſhe knew. It appeared from the furprize Vyvian expreſſed, that, ſo far from knowing any reaſon for the con- du&t of Montalbert, he was not certain of his being in England, and that all the intelligence he had gained, as to the re- fidence of Rofalie, came from Mrs. Lef- fington.

Claudine, who faw her miſtreſs incapa- ble of liſtening to this difcourfe, renewed her lamentations ; while Vyvian, eager and impatient, and not confidering the confequences, bade her call up the gen- tlemen below : an injun&tion which Clau- dine, as inconfiderate as himfelf, immedi- ately obeyed.

Rofalie, therefore, hardly opened her eyes after ſo unexpe&ted an appearance as that of Charles Vyvian, before they were ſtruck with the figure of William Lef- fington, who, though greatly altered ſince

ſhe

fhe faw him laft, fhe immediately knew:
but the fuddennefs of his appearance, the
diftrefs vifible in his countenance, and ftill
more in that of the ftranger who ftood by
him, with clapfed hands, and an expreffion
of mingled terror, pity, and affection,
filently gazing on her, amazed her fo
much, that fhe was incapable of afking
either who he was, or why he feemed fo
interefted in her fate?—She was incapable,
indeed, of fpeaking at all, but held out
her hand to Mr. Leffington, in a manner
which forcibly expreffed—" Oh! friend
and guide of my youth! why have you fo
long deferted your unhappy Rofalie?"

Leffington now fpoke to her.—" My
deareft friend! (faid he), my fweet Rofalie, you are ill!—you are unhappy!"

" I am, indeed," fhe would have anfwered, but fhe could not articulate the words.
Her attempt, however, had fomething fo
affecting in it, that the ftranger could no
longer reftrain the emotions which arofe
in his breaft; he burft into an agony of
tears, and, turning from her, exclaimed—

 " She

" She too is deftroyed—deftroyed as her mother was, by the accurfed houfe of Montalbert!——Yes!—the nephew refembles the uncle—he has murdered *my* daughter!"

Thefe ftrange exclamations ferved entirely to overcome the feeble fpirits of Rofalie; fhe no longer comprehended, and but indiftinctly heard, what paffed.—Leffington hung over her with the tendereft concern, while Vyvian walked about the room in great agitation; yet attempted to appeafe that of the ftranger, and now and then fpoke a broken fentence to Rofalie. It was evident, that far from relieving the fweet fufferer, for whom they were all interefted, by a continuation of this fcene, they did but increafe her anguifh, yet none of them had fufficient prefence of mind to remark this; and there was no woman about her, who had fenfe or obfervation enough, to advife them to withdraw till fhe could acquire more compofure.

The

The agitation of the stranger became more violent. It was Ormsby, the unfortunate father of Rosalie, who, having returned with an ample fortune from India, had been informed, on his first inquiries, that Mrs. Vyvian was dead. From Mrs. Lessington he had learned, that young Vyvian, her son, was, by a paper she wrote to him before her death, acquainted with the real relationship in which Rosalie stood to him, and with the circumstances that had rendered her marriage with his father a source of continual unhappiness.

Charles Vyvian, who had always loved his mother much better than his father, whose sole attachment to him originated in family pride, no sooner knew this history, than, with every attention that delicacy and duty required towards the character and memory of his mother, he sought, as soon as he returned to England, the family of Lessington. The eldest son, who was settled near Oxford, was more easily applied to than any other part of it. To him, therefore, Vyvian addressed him-

self,

felf, and thither alfo Mr. Ormfby was directed, when, on application to Mrs. Leffington, he found fhe was herfelf fettled
in the north. After an explanation between thefe gentlemen, they determined to
feek Rofalie together; and fet out for
Eaftbourne, without fufpecting that fhe
was fuffering under any other unhappinefs than that which arofe from a temporary feparation from her hufband; they
arrived at Eaftbourne, and found her emaciated by illnefs, injured in intellects by
grief, and incapable of feeling that por-
tion of happinefs and profperity, which,
they hoped, it would have been in their
power to offer her.

Ormfby, from the moment he had learned that he had a daughter living, who was
worthy, for her own fake, of the tendernefs he was difpofed to feel towards the
reprefentative of the woman he adored,
he cherifhed the moft flattering hopes of
happinefs with a lovely being, who would
recal continually to his mind the hours of
his early felicity, and gild the evening of

his

his life. He now found all vifionary blifs
vanifhed at once, and the bitternefs of his
difappointment was aggravated, when he
remembered that the blow, which had
murdered his happinefs a fecond time,
came from the fame family that had deftroyed it before. The injuries, the de-
ceptions, the tyranny, of Old Montalbert,
which had driven him from the bofom of
his firft Rofalie to exile and to forrow,
now feemed to be revived in the nephew
to rob him of all he had left; and, in the
anguifh of heart, which thefe thoughts
gave him, he forgot, that, by his unguard-
ed tranfports, he was deepening the wounds
he deplored. Such, however, were the
unhappy effects of his expreffions on the
bewildered mind of his daughter, who
catching from them fome vague ideas about
her mother, (whofe name he often repeated), though unable to follow the chain
of circumftances to which thefe expreffions alluded, that her fpirits were entirely
overcome; and, when he fondly called
her his daughter, his only hope on earth,

his

his poor unfortunate child! fhe was fo far from underftanding it was her father who fpoke to her, that fhe wildly fancied it was the fame perfon who had been fent by Montalbert to take her child from her. She fhuddered, therefore, as he approach- ed her; withdrew her hand from him, as he attempted to take it, and looking with wild and eager eyes towards Leffington, who engaged her notice more than Vyvian, fhe appeared filently to entreat that he would deliver her from the prefence of a perfon, of whom, was evident from her manner, fhe had conceived fome unfa- vourable impreffion.

Shocked by this conviction, and affured that her intellects were entirely gone, the unhappy father haftily left the room, and threw himfelf into a chair in the parlour below, where he gave way to the anguifh of his foul.

The fight of Rofalie, though fhe refem- bled her mother more by her air and voice than by any pofitive likenefs of features, had brought to his mind a thoufand

fand tender recollections; and, in believing her irreparably hurt both in her understanding and constitution, he felt as if the wounds that had been so long healing, after his separation from her mother, were now torn open afresh; and the happiness which he had fondly hoped might gild the evening of his life seemed now vanished for ever.—Why Montalbert had left Rosalie, or why he had so cruelly taken her child from her, he could not imagine. Vyvian had learned these particulars from Claudine, and had unguardedly communicated them to the rest; but as Claudine was herself ignorant of his motives, she could only relate the facts, and Mr. Ormsby, never disposed to think favourably of the family of Montalbert, could see nothing in such actions but an hereditary depravity and malignity, which he execrated. It was not long before Vyvian joined him in the parlour. Ormsby said little to him of the resolution he was silently forming, while Vyvian, who was extremely hurt at the situation of Rosalie,

L 4   whom

whom he had ever tenderly loved, believing
it impoffible that Montalbert could act, as
he was reprefented to have done, without
fome very ftrange mifunderftanding, determined to fet out immediately in queft of
him, and, reprefenting the fituation of his
wife, endeavour to develope the caufe of
his having thrown her into it by his rafh
and unkind conduct.

Mr. Leffington, in the mean time, was
attempting to footh and appeafe the trou-
bled mind of his ever-beloved Rofalie, in
hopes of learning and of alleviating her
diftrefs. He at length fucceeded fo far,
as to procure from her the words " Yes! "
or " No!" to fome of the queftions he put
to her; but to others fhe remained filent,
or anfwered only by a deep figh. Finding
he could gain, therefore, but little information, though he ftaid with her near half
an hour longer than the other two gentlemen, he left her, faying he would return to
her immediately, and rejoined his diftreffed
friends below.

Some

Some converfation there paffed between them, in which the calmnefs of Mr. Leffington was happily oppofed to the agitation of a father oppreffed with forrow, and the natural vivacity of Vyvian, who now felt difpofed to quarrel with his coufin, and now to account for conduct which feemed to him unpardonable, if fome reafon could not be given for it.

Leffington, whofe attachment to Rofalie had grown up with him, liftened to each of them with patience, but acquiefced in neither of their plans. That of Mr. Ormfby, though he did not openly avow it, was to feek Montalbert, demand an explanation of his conduct, and, if he could not give fome very good reafon for meafures fo harfh and violent as he had adopted, to demand of him the fatisfaction due to the injured honour and peace of the unfortunate Rofalie. Leffington perfectly underftood this by the half fentences and angry expreffions of Ormfby, and he faw the neceffity of preventing a meafure which muft involve the object of his fo-

licitude

licitude in yet deeper calamity. It was not eafy, in the prefent agitated ftate of his mind, to fay any thing that would not rather irritate than footh, and, therefore, Leffington affected to attend rather to the project of Vyvian, who propofed fetting out immediately to find Montalbert, and endeavour to clear up whatever miftake had given rife to proceedings fo unlike the ufual tenor of his conduct.

Though Leffington was clearly of opinion that Vyvian was not the propereft perfon to engage in this explanation, yet, as he hoped to obtain Ormfby's patience while he was about it, and that fomething might happen in the mean time to clear up the darknefs in which they were involved, he feemed to agree to Vyvian's departure, ftill, however, with coldnefs and reluctance, and as if he meditated on fome fcheme which he thought more eligible. At this inftant Lady Llancarrick and Mifs Gillman appeared; the former having heard of the arrival of the ftrangers, introduced herfelf to them as the dear friend

of

of Mrs. Sheffield, and, as fuch, it feemed
probable that fhe could give them information as to the caufe of the appearances which had fo greatly diftreffed them.
The change of name, which, though Mrs.
Leffington had mentioned it, had been
hardly attended to before, now feemed to
ftrike Mr. Ormfby as if it were entirely
new to him——Why fhould his daughter
have changed her name?—An appearance
of concealment is always injurious. It
might, however, be at the defire of her
hufband, fince their marriage was clan-
deftine. This reflection fatisfied his mind
for a moment as to that circumftance, but,
as Mr. Leffington and Mr. Vyvian continued to converfe one with Lady Llancarrick and the other with Mifs Gillman,
Mr. Ormfby, who liftened to them alternately, found fo many obfcure hints, or
evafive anfwers in their converfation, and
thought them women whofe acquaintance
feemed fo little creditable to his daughter,
that his uneafinefs became infupportable.

L 6   He

He dreaded left in the conduct of Rofalie he fhould find but too ftrong a juftification of that of Montalbert. This idea
was infinitely more painful to him than to
believe her innocent and fuffering only
from mifapprehenfion or injuftice, and
unable to bear the diftrefs of mind, which
every moment increafed, he ftarted up,
and, leaving the room, walked up a lane
near the houfe, which he traverfed with
hafty and uncertain fteps while the conference lafted, which had already given
him fo much uneafinefs.

Before that conference ended, the conviction that both Leffington and Vyvian
had entertained of the perfect and unim-
peachable difcretion of Rofalie was cruelly fhaken. They had learned from Lady
Llancarrick, who either could not or would
not conceal any thing fhe knew, that, under a feigned name herfelf, and under the
protection of a young man of the name of
Walfingham, fhe had appeared at the village, where fhe had lived fince in a retired

tired way, but frequently receiving him at her houfe, and, as it was generally underftood, fupported by him.

To two young men, who knew nothing of the extraordinary chain of events which had feparated Rofalie from Montalbert, (for Vyvian had paffed eighteen months in the German Courts, from whence he had come to England only three months before this period), thefe circumftances could not fail of having a very unfavourable appearance. Vyvian, as foon as the ladies from whom they had gathered this intelligence were gone, talked of feeking this Mr. Walfingham, and demanding an explanation of him; a fcheme which appeared to Leffington to be more pregnant with mifchief than even that propofed by Ormfby. They now went in fearch of the latter, and found him overwhelmed with forrow and anxiety. The ftate in which his daughter was, gave him the moft acute pain, which was infinitely increafed by the dread he now entertained as to her conduct.—What Leffington and Vyvian had to fay, though

the

the former foftened it all he could, was but ill calculated to appeafe thefe fears; and a conflict now arofe in the breaft of the unhappy father, between his wifh to return to, and, if poffible, comfort his af-flicted child, and his reluctance even to fee her, if it could be true that fhe had de-ferted her hufband, and difgraced herfelf.

He determined, however, once more to fee her, and to fee her alone. He found, on entering her apartment, that all the fymptoms that feemed to have a little fub-fided, while fhe had been flattered with hopes of hearing news of her child, had fince returned with renewed violence; a deadly palenefs overfpread her counte-nance, and a fever feemed to devour her. If Claudine fpoke to her, fhe anfwered only by a deep figh. and when fhe became fenfible that a ftranger was in the room, and opening her eyes faw Ormfby, fhe caft a reproaching look towards Claudine, waved with her hand for him to leave her, and then, covering her face with her hand-kerchief, funk into filence, from which

not

not even the voice of Leffington could
roufe her:—he, at the defire of Mr. Ormfby,.
went to her, fpoke to her, and entreated
her to attend to her own health, to the
anxiety of her friends; he even named
her father to her, but he could obtain no
other anfwer, than a faint entreaty that he
would leave to her deftiny a creature born
only to be miferable. At length, fhe faid,.
" My father!—alas! *I* have no father!—
Do not mock me! I never faw a father!—
I had a hufband—indeed I had a child,.
but both are gone, and I am now a wretched outcaft?"

" Have you not friends, Rofalie?—
(Leffington then ventured to fay)—Surely
there are fome in whom you place confidence and friendfhip, though you deny
it to him whom you once loved to call
by the tender name of brother?"

To this it feemed as if fhe was either
unable or unwilling to anfwer directly;
for again, with a deep drawn figh, and in
a half-ftifled voice, fhe faid, " You—you
are my brother ftill, William, if you do

not

not difdain the title—and then I fhall not be——as, indeed, I think myfelf now—quite—quite friendlefs ! "

She was now again fenfible, yet Leffington doubted whether it was a proper hour to fpeak to her of her father, fince every time he had either fpoken to her, or been named to her, her ideas feemed to have taken a confufed flight, from whence it was not very eafy to recal them; and though Mr. Ormfby earneftly wifhed fhe might be made to underftand that he was her father, yet Leffington faw her mind fo fhaken by trying to imprefs on it what her mother had, he believed, never fully related to her, that he dreaded left fuch an attempt now might be of the worft confequences.

All he judged prudent to do, therefore, was to footh her mind as much as he could for that night, and perfuade her father to leave her. This, though not without difficulty, he effected. Ormfby went again with him to the parlour, whither the landlady was now fummoned to give information

tion where the beſt phyſician in the neighbourhood was to be obtained.

A meſſenger was diſpatched for one, but
hardly was he gone, and Leſſington entering into converſation with his two friends
on what he thought was propereſt to be
done, when a ſervant on horſeback brought
a letter, directed for Mrs. Sheffield, which,
he ſaid, required an immediate anſwer.—
On being queſtioned by Mr. Vyvian who
it was from, the man anſwered inſolently
enough, " That he had no orders to tell
that, unleſs to the lady herſelf; but that,
for his part, he was never aſhamed of his
maſter's name—it came from Squire Walſingham."

Ormſby, who ſaw in the name of Walſingham, and in ſuch a correſpondence,
a confirmation of all the fears that had aſ-
ſailed him for the reputation and peace
of his daughter, determined to open this
letter. Leſſington at firſt doubted how
far this might be juſtifiable; but yielding
at length to the authority of a father, the
letter was opened, and, to the aſtoniſhment

and

and indignation of the parties, was found to contain thefe words————

" MADAM,

" A gentleman of the name of Mon-talbert has taken the trouble to write to me, on a fuppofition of my being a much more fortunate man than I have ever fuf-pected myfelf to be. He wifhes me to meet him at my own time and place, to explain to him my pretenfions to the very great favours which he affures me you have honoured me with, as well in a cer-tain long voyage, which it feems we made together, as fince our return to England, where he affirms you have remained under my protection.

" Having hinted to him that I am per-fectly unconfcious of all this, I have re-ceived a fecond letter, couched in terms which do not generally pafs unnoticed be-tween gentlemen. Now, Madam, if I muft rifk the penalty, it is but juft that I fhould be made confcious of the happy trefpafs by which I have incurred it; when

I am,

I am perfuaded I fhall meet with exultation whatever may happen; or if it hitherto exifts only in the imagination of my correfpondent, I am, neverthelefs, ready to meet him as he defires, provided that before I become *his* adverfary, you will permit me to affume the pleafing and honourable title of your champion.

" But, as no time is to be loft, I await your anfwer with extrême impatience, flattering myfelf it will bring permiffion to throw himfelf at your feet, one who is,

Dear Madam,
Your moft devoted fervant,
S. WALSINGHAM."

Vyvian had no fooner heard the contents of this extraordinary billet, than he flew out of the room to find the fervant that had brought it, for it appeared as if the writer of it was waiting fomewhere in the neighbourhood, and he was at all events refolved to find him.

Of Mr. Walfingham, neither Ormfby, Vyvian, nor Leffington knew any thing but

the

the name ; and this letter, of whatever nature might have been his acquaintance with
Rofalie, having certainly the air of an infult, was not calculated to give them a
favourable opinion of him. None of them
could help feeing, that a meeting between
him and Montalbert muft be attended with
fatal confequences, if not to the life of
either, at leaft to the honour of the unfortunate young woman, who was the caufe
of their quarrel. Vyvian, breathing nothing but vengeance againft a man capable
of writing fuch a letter, would liften to
nothing that Leffington could fay ; and
Ormfby, loft in bewildering conjectures,
but more uneafy than ever, determined at
length to purfue his original plan of finding Montalbert ; and, having learned the
caufe of his conduct, and of the prefent
extraordinary letter, to take Rofalie and
conceal her in fome obfcure retreat if fhe
was guilty ; or, if fhe was innocent, to
vindicate that innocence in the face of the
world. It was, however, neceffary for him
to await the arrival of the phyfician who
was

was fent for, as it was certain the perfonal
fufferings of his unhappy daughter became
every hour more alarming. Leffington,
with the moſt patient pity both for Ormſby
and his child, remained with him ; but his
arguments had no longer any effect on the
impetuofity of Vyvian, who having learned, from the fervant he had queſtioned,
that Mr. Walfingham was at Brightelm-
ſtone, fet off thither in a poſt chaife, attended only by his fervant, affuring his
friends that he had no defign of taking the
refentment of Montalbert out of his hands ;
but that he was determined to clear up this
extraordinary bufinefs in fome way or other,
and that they fhould hear of him in a very
few hours.

With thefe affurances, fince he would
hear nothing Ormſby or Leffington could
fay to urge remaining with them, they were
compelled to fuffer him to depart.

CHAP.

CHAP. XXXVI.

IT was already late in the evening, and Ormfby and Leffington awaited in the moft diftreffing fufpenfe the arrival of the phyfician they expected; the meffenger fent to him having returned, to fay he would be with them as foon as poffible. Rofalie, though ftill confcious of, and grateful for the attentions of Leffington, feemed too ill to enter into converfation or explanation of any kind. But at length in attempting to footh and to reafon with her, he prevailed upon her to fay, that fhe fhould die contented, and even prefer death, if fhe could but fee her child once more, and afk his father's protection for him. This was more than fhe had yet coherently faid; and Leffington, who was now alone by her bed-fide, made an effort

to

to carry the converfation farther. "And why, my dear Rofalie," faid he, "why do you doubt his protecting his fon? Since he has taken him from you, however unkind that ftep may have been, as far as it regards you, Mr. Montalbert had probably no other defign than to take care of him, and give him a father's protection."—"Good God!" exclaimed Rofalie, "can you, my dear Sir, believe that he could have been guilty of fo very cruel an action, as tearing him from me, had he not determined to deftroy me, and to erafe all recollection of a marriage, which he probably repents, and is afhamed of?—His mother, his cruel mother, and his treacherous friend Alozzi"—fhe here paufed a moment, unable to go on—"have prevailed on him to abandon me. Perhaps too, fome newer attachment . . . . for I can never think that *they* alone could influence him—fome newer attachment." She could proceed no farther; the idea was too cruel to be fupported; and her voice became inarticulate through the violence of her emotions.

Leffington had never heard her fpeak fo much, and fo confiftently before, and greatly as he faw fhe was affected, he yet hoped that tears might rather relieve than injure her; he therefore ventured, after waiting a moment that fhe might recover herfelf, to go on.

" Perhaps, my dear Rofalie, neither of thefe caufes may have occafioned the eftrangement you deplore.—Perhaps, . . . forgive me if I feem to impute to you what you may be, and I believe are incapable of—but poffibly fome *unintentional* indifcretion on your part may have been exaggerated and mifreprefented.—Montalbert may have conceived himfelf injured by your conduct, and has rafhly treated you as culpable, without hearing your juftification."

Rofalie paufing a moment, as if to recollect her agitated fpirits, raifed herfelf on one arm, and with her other hand taking the hand of Leffington, fhe faid in
a low

a low, yet folemn voice, " My dear brother! as there is truth in Heaven, I was
never guilty of the flighteft deviation from
my duty, even in idea :—Montalbert muft
know my heart too well to fuppofe it.—I
long doubted of his exiftence; for you
know how we were feparated.—Yet never,
Oh! no never did my heart wander from
its faith and affection to him!"

" I do believe you, my poor Rofalie,"
faid Leffington, " I fincerely believe you,
though *how*, or even how long you were
feparated, I am totally ignorant."

" I have papers that will explain it to
you, my William, but I feel that it muft
be when I am no more; then Claudine
fhall deliver you a fmall box, in which you
will find a journal of my unhappy life,
while I was able to keep a journal.—Yet
a little, and I fhall need no other juftification to Montalbert.—When he finds
that he has deftroyed me, it is he, poor
man, who will want confolation—who will
be an object of pity."

Rosalie spoke slowly, and with difficulty, and in a weak, faint voice; yet her anxious father, who had glided into the room, heard her distinctly; and as she had never appeared to him so collected before, he was tremblingly solicitous for her to learn that he lived, and sought only to protect her:—Like one who sees his sole treasure half escaped from an abyss, yet knows it is not quite in safety, and dreads to see it again snatched from his uncertain grasp. So Ormsby seemed lost in the contrariety of emotions he felt: he softly approached Lessington, and in a whisper besought him to speak to Rosalie of her father. But, however carefully he uttered this, his daughter heard some words, which as every thing now hurried and alarmed her, made her hastily put aside the curtain.

The amazement, not unmingled with some degree of apprehension, which she expressed on seeing a stranger, was a proof how little she remembered of what had passed before: Ormsby, unable to command his emotion, sobbed aloud. As

Stooping

ftooping over her, he took her pale and emaciated hands; " Rofalie!" cried he, " dear reprefentative of the moft beloved, and moft injured of women—Speak to me —Speak to, and acknowledge your un-happy father!" The look with which fhe regarded him alarmed Leffington, who faid, " My dear Rofalie, your mother has left with Vyvian papers, in which it is de-clared, that before your marriage fhe dif-covered to you the myftery of your birth, and why it was that you paffed as the child of my parents, while your own were con-cealed.—Recollect, my fweet friend, all that your dear mother faid to you; and then you will at once underftand how it is that your father, who very lately arrived from the Eaft Indies, now haftens to claim the only treafure his fate has left him." All the particulars indeed that her mother had related at that moment returned to her mind: her heart acknowledged the dear tie that was now offered to it; fhe raifed her languid frame, and would have thrown herfelf into the arms of Ormfby,

but

but her ftrength failed her—fhe was only able to pronounce " My father," before fhe funk down in the fame ftate of weak-nefs which had often appeared fo alarm-ing—but before Ormfby or Leffington could conjecture how they fhould repair the imprudence they had thus been guilty of, the phyfician they expected arrived.

It was hardly poffible that he could come at a more unfavourable time to judge of his patient: he found her indeed in a ftate, which, as the reafon of her violent and extraordinary emotion could not be entirely explained, gave him an opinion of her danger, even beyond the truth; and when he retired with her father and Mr. Leffington, he expreffed fuch fears as to the event of her illnefs, that Ormfby, half frantic, could hardly be prevented from fetting out for London immediately, and bringing down, at any expence, the moft eminent phyfician, who could be prevailed upon to take the journey. Leffington faw that this would anfwer no purpofe, fince if Rofalie was in fo hazardous a ftate, as

fhe

she was believed to be, it would be too late to expect relief from affiftance that was to come fo far. He thought it better to engage the gentleman now with them to remain all night, and to await the event of the morning; and this with fome diffi-culty he accomplifhed.

The fever which preyed upon Rofalie, and which had originated folely in anguifh of mind, increafed during this miferable night; but it feemed no longer to affect her intellects: amid variety of pain, her fenfes were fo clear, that fhe repeated to Claudine what fhe had faid relative to the box which was to be given to her friends. She told her too, that it was her father who was below, and that fhe had never feen him before, but forbore any other explanation. Ormfby and Leffington, who could neither of them fleep, and who did not indeed attempt going to bed, had vifited her room feveral times during the night, and flattered themfelves from thefe fymptoms that fhe was amending: but when Dr. G. faw her at an early hour of

the

the morning, he thought her fever higher, and the whole houfe was in confternation and defpair.

It was towards noon—the phyfician was gone, having promifed to return in the evening. Ormfby and Leffington, as the fuffering patient was apparently fleeping, had walked out to relieve their fatigued and anxious fpirits by the air, and having remained out about half an hour, they were met, juft as they entered the houfe, by Claudine: who, with expreffions of great joy in her countenance, told them, in her broken Englifh, " That Mr. Walfingham was come; Le bon Walfingham, l'excellent Ami de fa chere Maitreffe;" for all that, and more his generofity to her, had made him appear to Claudine. Claudine therefore was very much furprifed and mortified to find, that the intelligence fhe was eager to communicate was fo far from giving pleafure to either of the gentlemen, that they advanced towards the parlour, where fhe had told them Mr. Walfingham

was

was, with evident marks of anger in their countenance and manner.

The letter they had feen addreffed to Rofalie, impreffed them with the moft un-favourable idea of the perfon they were going to meet: Ormfby, fhocked at his arrival, which feemed a confirmation of fears in regard to the conduct of his daugh-ter, which had been a while fufpended by fears for her health, was tempted to affront him even on the firft moment of meeting him; and it was with difficulty he was diverted from this petulance by Leffington, who faid, as they were entering the houfe, " I own I cannot fee, my good Sir, what we fhall gain by preventing an explanation from this young man, which he will cer-tainly not give us, if we directly infult him: whereas, if there is any miftake in all this (as I cannot but believe there is), a little coolnefs may ferve, if not to make us eafy, at leaft to produce fuch an ex-planation as will direct our refentment. Above all things, it feems to me neceffary

to

to avoid every thing like violence in this small houfe, if you would not endanger yet more the life of your daughter."

Ormfby felt the reafonablenefs of this remonftrance, and checked his own feelings as much as poffible, though his countenance and air expreffed them but too forcibly. If thefe gentlemen were aftonifhed at his appearance, after fuch a letter as he had written, they were ftill more fo, to find him a young man of a very different appearance to what they had figured to themfelves the writer of fo impertinent a letter muft be.

Walfingham, unconfcious of any offence, and rather fuppofing he fhould be received as the friend and protector of Rofalie, (for Claudine had explained who thefe gentlemen were) was immediately repulfed by the angry countenance of the elder gentleman, and the cold and diftant bow of the other. He advanced, however, and in that graceful manner which his habitual dejection rather made more interefting, he expreffed the extreme con-

cern

cern he felt at hearing of the indifpofition of Mrs. Montalbert. Yet how much fatis-faction it gave him, (and he bowed to Ormfby as he fpoke), to learn that fhe was happy in the tender attentions of a father. " If you *know* me, Sir," faid Ormfby, " you ought to know and to feel, that your prefence here is an infult which muft de-ferve the deepeft refentment of injured honour. Are you come, Sir, to over-whelm with fhame my unfortunate daugh-ter in her laft hours? Are you come to triumph over a miferable family, whom you have ruined in their fame, and in their happinefs?" All the paffions of an injured father, combined in the bofom of Ormfby, who trembling, and for a moment de-prived of breath, gave Walfingham (as he ftood petrified by fuch an addrefs), time to fay—

" *Am* I come, Sir, with *this* defign? am I come with *any* defign injurious to the peace and honour of Mrs. Montalbert? Certainly not. You muft greatly have miftaken me, if you fuppofe it." Ormfby,

M 5   by

by a motion of his head and hand, expreffed what he could not at that moment
find words to utter: while Leffington,
taking advantage of this involuntary filence, faid, " After fuch a letter, Sir, as
that with which you have affronted Mrs.
Montalbert, and, through her, all her family, all her friends, you muft fuppofe . . . . . ."

" A letter, Sir," interrupted Walfingham, " a letter from me? and infulting
Mrs. Montalbert? That is a charge which
I own I am not prepared to anfwer. I
have moft certainly never written to Mrs.
Montalbert fince I had the honour of feeing
her laft."

Ormfby, naturally violent, yet fubdued
by time and trouble, was fo overcome,
that he had thrown himfelf half fuffocated
into a chair. Leffington, more mafter of
himfelf, continued to fpeak for him.

" The letter, Sir, however, that we received, can admit of no excufe : you have
feen or heard of Mr. Montalbert?"

" Pardon

" Pardon me, Sir, I have done nei-ther—I did not even know he was in England."

The countenance of Walfingham underwent a vifible change as he faid this; Leffington failed not to remark it, but imputed it to emotions very different from thofe that Walfingham felt while he continued fo fpeak.

" No, Sir, I did not even know Mr. Montalbert was come to England; but as it appears that he is, may I requeſt the favour of a direction to him? You will alfo oblige me by fhewing me the letter, which I am fuppofed to have written to his wife, if fhe is, as I fear, too ill to admit of my applying to her for it perfonally."

The emotion of Walfingham increafed; he turned very pale, and his lips trembled.

" I have not got the letter," faid Ormfby, " nor has my daughter ever feen it; Mr. Vyvian has taken it with him to Brighthelmftone, where your fervant told us you were to be found, in order to demand an explanation."

M 6

" My

" *My fervant!*" exclaimed Walfingham, more and more furprifed; " there is certainly fome ftrange miftake in all this. Pray, Sir, with what name was it figned?" Leffington then anfwering that it was " S. Walfingham." Walfingham began immediately to fufpect the truth; but when Leffington explained to him the contents of this letter, and that they evidently alluded to a demand of fatisfaction, which the writer of it had received from Montalbert; and when he alfo faid that Vyvian had left them the preceding evening in the full determination to have a meeting with Mr. Walfingham, all the mifchief which might happen between Montalbert, Vyvian, and his gay, fafhionable coufin (from whom he now eafily underftood the letter came), occurred in an inftant to his mind. He faw that the death of one of them, perhaps of more, was likely to follow from the mere miftake of a name. He faw the extreme concern which Rofalie might feel, if any evil fhould happen even to a ftranger, whofe offence towards her was at leaft palliated

liated by ignorance; but fhould Montalbert or Vyvian be wounded, or fall, the
confequences to her muſt be ſtill more
dreadful.

All this no fooner ſtruck Walfingham,
than he explained as clearly as he could the
nature of his apprehenſions to Leſſington,
who faw at once that they were too well
grounded, for Walfingham defcribed his
relation as raſh, haughty, and violent;-
one who could be much more likely to
retort any affront with intereſt, than to en-
quire the ground on which it was given.
Ormſby and Leſſington were alfo well
aſſured that Vyvian was irritable, proud,
and impatient; and though neither of them
were perfonally acquainted with Montalbert, they had no reafon to believe, from
all they had heard of him, that he was by
any means of a calmer difpofition. A
collufion then between thefe three, or
even any two of thefe fiery fpirits, could
hardly fail of producing fome fatal event.

The generous mind and excellent heart
of Walfingham were never more confpi-

cuous than at this moment. Without
feeming to advert to the challenge, which
it was certain Montalbert had fent to his
coufin, while intending it for him—without any menace, or even hint of his refentment, he expreffed nothing but a wifh
to go immediately in purfuit of the parties,
and endeavour to prevent a meeting, from
which fo much was to be dreaded. It was
not till after a fevere ftruggle, however,
that he could determine to quit the houfe,
not only without feeing Rofalie, but without enquiring after her health, or the circumftances which had deprived her of it
fo fuddenly. Claudine had told him
enough to convince him that Montalbert
had been actuated by jealoufy, and he
fuppofed the objeft of that jealoufy was
himfelf.—A thoufand painful thoughts
crowded upon his heart—the hufband of
Rofalie was returned:—No doubt, therefore, remained of his exiftence; and it
became more than ever prudent for the
ill-ftarred Walfingham to ftifle the growing
affection which muft now be utterly hopelefs.—

lefs.—But fo much did that affection par-
take of his noble fpirit, that the happinefs
and the peace of Rofalie were infinitely
dearer to him than his own, and he flew
to fave the hufband, whofe life was between him and thofe hopes which, in de-
fpite of reafon, he had at times indulged.

If his tafk was in this refpect painful,
it was hardly lefs fo in what related to Mr.
Ormfby; though the matter of the letter
was cleared up, he faw, that the father of
Rofalie regarded him as one who had been
the caufe of Montalbert's eftrangement
from her; that long and difagreeable ex-
planations muft take place, and that he
could hardly hope to be received even
as the friend of her to whom he felt fuch
painful partiality.—Ormfby, while he anx-
ioufly haftened his departure, treated him
with coolnefs, almoft with incivility; but
Leffington, with milder manners, was more
ready to believe that no blame could at-
tach to the conduct of Rofalie in regard
to him. Walfingham faw enough to give
him great fears on her account; and with

a

a heart penetrated by forrow, he fet out poft to overtake Vyvian, and, if poffible, meet Montalbert, who, from the fubftance of his relation's letter which Leffington repeated to Walfingham, was, he con.. cluded, either at Brighthelmftone, or in its neighbourhood, waiting the rendezvous which he had demanded.

The wild indifcretion of Claudine had communicated to her miftrefs the arrival of Walfingham ; and though her regard for him was as pure and innocent as that which fhe felt for either of thofe whom fhe had learned to confider as her brothers, yet fhe fuffered extremely when fhe found he was gone, and had not feen her: not only becaufe fhe was fure it would give him pain, but becaufe it convinced her that the generous protection he had offered her had been the caufe of his becoming fufpected by thofe who ought to have felt the greateft obligation towards him; and becaufe fhe dreaded left he fhould be involved in farther difficulties on her account.—She did not indeed know how

near

near he already was to the dangers she apprehended for him.

Ill as Rofalie was, however, she was not fo enervated in mind as in body; and after hearing from Claudine an account of Walfingham's departure, and all she had collected or fancied of the converfation while he ftaid, she fummoned refolution enough to determine upon putting into Leffington's hands the account she had kept of every event, from her arrival at Naples to the moment when she fo unexpectedly met with a friend and protector in Walfingham, and was delivered almoft by a miracle from her hopelefs confinement. During her voyages she had alfo made memorandums of every occurrence, and fince her refidence at Eaftbourne she had returned to her journal, and related the events of her life, monotonous as they were, in the flattering hope that Montalbert might one day go over them, and that they might bear teftimony to her unceafing attachment to him, and to her duty.

In

In the eḟ ̇ions of an ingenuous and unadulterated mind there is always a simplicity of character, which at once evinces the truth of whatever it relates. Though Rofalie thought not of that, fhe yet felt, that if once Montalbert could be prevailed upon to read her narrative, all that had befallen her would be explained.——Shocked as fhe was at his cruel conduct towards her, and defpairing ever to fee him more, fhe had directed that thefe papers might not be delivered till after her death, which fhe believed to be nearly approaching; but as from what Mr. Leffington had faid to her, from the fudden appearance of Walfingham, his departure without feeing her, and from all that Claudine had told her, of the manner and countenance of Mr. Ormfby, Rofalie had but too much reafon to think the generous friendfhip of Walfingham towards her might endanger his life, fhe rallied her feeble and fainting fpirits to confider how it was poffible to avert the dreaded evil. She faw this could only be done by her putting into the hands

of

of Leffington thefe proofs of Walfingham's
difinterefted friendfhip, and leaving him
to act as fhe knew his own prudence and
fenfe would dictate.

CHAP. XXXVII.

CLAUDINE went down by the direction of her miſtreſs, who requeſted to ſee Mr. Leſſington. On his entering the room, he found her raiſed in the bed by pillars; her countenance was very much changed for the worſe ſince he was with her laſt, and her pale hands trembled while ſhe ſorted ſome packets of papers tied with ribands, which ſhe took out of two boxes that were before her.

She looked at him, but did not ſpeak. It, therefore, immediately occurred to Leſſington, that Claudine had informed her of Walſingham's arrival and departure; and he felt confuſed and diſtreſſed, not knowing how he could avoid giving the ſorrowful information ſhe would ſeek.—— Roſalie, on her part, not only feared to

aſk

afk any queftions, but dreaded to hear
what had paffed—for fhe was now poffeffed
of recolleſtion enough to advert to all that
Leffington had faid, and knew that Walfingham was an objeſt of fufpicion to him
and Mr. Ormfby : nor could fhe doubt
but that the conduſt of her hufband had
been occafioned by the fame miftruft.—
The appearance, therefore, of Walfingham, muft undoubtedly have deepened
all thefe ill impreffions, and Rofalie could
not think upon them without the moft acute
pain, fince it was but too probable that
the generous and difintereſted friendfhip
of Walfingham had brought upon him
treatment he little deferved, and which
fhe thought him very unlikely to bear patiently. If thefe fears and conjeſtures
were almoft infupportable, what would fhe
have fuffered, had fhe known how much
of the evil fhe apprehended was already
realized; while Walfingham, unweared in
generofity, was more than ever entitled to
her gratitude and regard.

Her

Her ſickened ſoul, where indeed reſted the cauſe of all her complaints, ſo far af-fected her enfeebled frame, that, when ſhe would have explained to Leſſington the nature of the papers ſhe put into his hands, by relating her ſituation at the va-rious times on which they had been writ-ten, ſhe could hardly finiſh even a ſen-tence—but, putting the packets into his hands, ſhe faintly bade him read them in the order in which they were tied.—— " You, and my poor father, (ſaid ſhe, in a faint voice), will find that your unhappy Roſalie has done nothing which ought to make you aſhamed of the affection you have felt for her.... Vindicate my honour, William !—reſcue my memory from re-proach !—and, for the ſake of my dear, dear boy, convince his father that I die innocent of all reproach, and that even in death I bleſs and love him." - - - - - - - - She would have ſaid more, but put her hand to her forehead, and ſignified that ſhe could not.

Leſſington,

Leffington, affected even to tears and fobs, could not command himfelf fufficiently to fpeak. The fight of his emotion added frefh pangs to what fhe endured, when, waving her hand, fhe feemed to entreat him to leave her, and he filently obeyed.

It was fome time before he could recover himfelf enough to read aloud the melancholy narrative thus entrufted to him, to which Mr. Ormfby liftened with anxious yet gloomy attention. When they had arrived at that part of the journal, written on board the fhip which brought her to England, they faw far enough into her ftory to be convinced that the meeting of Rofalie with Walfingham was entirely accidental; that fhe could not have acted otherwife than fhe did, and that the conduct of Walfingham had been that of the moft generous and difinterefted of friends: little, therefore, remained neceffary for the entire vindication of both parties, but to remove the falfe impreffions given by Lady - Llancarrick and her friend, that they had
refided

refided together at Eaftbourne, which, though thofe amiable ladies had not af-ferted, they had fpoken of in fuch a man-ner as to leave little doubt of the fact.

Jealous for the honour of his daughter, which her own artlefs narrative had nearly cleared, (fo powerful is fimple truth), Ormfby now preffed eagerly to have all his remaining doubts fatisfied. Though Claudine could not keep up a regular dialogue, fhe could make herfelf under-ftood when plain queftions only were put to her. Ormfby, with that trembling ap-prehenfion which is felt by thofe who dread the refult of an inquiry which they are yet determined to make, called her into the room, and, with the affiftance of Leffington, had already convinced him-felf, that Mr. Walfingham had acted with the utmoft delicacy and propriety in re-gard to Rofalie, when a poft chaife and four, the horfes extremely fatigued, drove up to the door, and a gentleman, unknown to both Ormfby and Leffington, entered the room.

Pale,

Pale, his hair in diforder, his eyes wild, and his whole perfon expreffive of hafte and diftrefs, he uttered fomething, in a manner fo incoherent, that neither of them underftood him. He faw they did not; and, throwing himfelf into a chair, he faid, " I fuppofe I fpeak to Mr. Ormfby and Mr. Leffington. . . . . I imagine, Sir, (addreffing himfelf to the former)—I imagine your daughter is here ? "

Ormfby, alarmed and amazed, hefitated a moment, hardly knowing what to fay. The ftranger, without waiting for his anfwer, continued to fpeak————

" I know not whether you fee before you the moft injured, or the moft guilty, of men———I only know that I am the moft wretched ! "

" It is Mr. Montalbert, I believe, to whom I fpeak ! (faid Leffington).—It is long, very long, fince I faw you laft, Sir— and I fear - - - - - - -"

" You fear, and with but too much reafon, (faid Montalbert, interrupting him), that our meeting now can only be pro-

du_ctive of pain.......Vyvian has told
me --------"

"You have feen Vyvian then?" inquired Leffington.

"I faw him, but not till it was too late.
He is gone in fearch of another man of
the fame name as him whom _I_ moft unfor-
tunately met—and -------"

"Good God! (exclaimed Ormfby)—
you have met then with that Walfingham,
to whom Rofalie owes her fafety, perhaps
her life, and you have had the cruelty,
the rafhnefs -------"

"To kill him!" cried Montalbert with
fiercenefs, and in a tone that re-echoed
through the houfe.

Claudine, on the firft appearance of
Montalbert, whom fhe had never feen before, had liftened at the door of the room,
which was left half open; fhe heard this
terrible fpeech, and, fhrieking aloud, ran
up ftairs, but before fhe reached the door
of her lady's room, fhe fell down in a
fort of fit, fobbing and fcreaming aloud.
This was not wanting to terrify the unhappy

happy Rosalie; for tremblingly alive to every alarm since her child had been torn from her, there was seldom any thing passed in the house to which she did not listen. She heard the stopping of a carriage, the entrance of a person into the parlour, and soon after the voice of Montalbert, uttering the dreadful sentence—" I have killed him!"—struck her ears; then the shrieks of Claudine, who seemed to be immediately at her door—desperation lent her strength.

She had on a loose dressing gown, when throwing herself out of the bed, and holding by the furniture, for she was unable to move without such help, she reached the door of her apartment. Claudine weak, and at that moment incapable of exercising the very little judgement she ever possessed, continued to intercept the way, having thrown herself down on the stairs. Rosalie, leaning against the door-case, attempted, but in vain, to obtain an answer; and her increasing terrors threatened every instant to deprive her of the

N 2 little

little ftrength fhe had thus collected, when
Leffington, aware of the fad effect that
fuch a noife in the houfe muft have, fuddenly quitted Montalbert, without ftaying
to hear all he had to relate, and haftened
up ftairs, in hopes of appeafing the foolifh
maid, and accounting to Rofalie for the
alarm in fome way which might not deftroy her at once; to his utter aftonifh-
ment he found her out of her bed, looking
more dead than alive, and juft finking to
the ground as he fprang forward, and
caught her in his arms, then carrying her
into her room, he placed her in a chair,
and rang for affiftance, for he believed her
dying, and forgot, in that moment, every
thing elfe.

The confequence of his violence, however, was, that the father and hufband of
Rofalie rufhed alfo into the room, where
Leffington, fupporting her head, and cha-
fing her hands, continued to implore that
affiftance which none had the prefence of
mind to give. Some perfon, however,
had by this time fetched the apothecary,
and

and the ufual remedies being adminiftered, Rofalie feemed to be recovering. It was then, at the earneft entreaties of Leffington, that Montalbert and Ormfby were prevailed upon to go out of the room, and Leffington foon after followed them, declaring that his fifter (for fo he always called her) was much better, and, if left to the women for a little while, would foon be entirely recovered. It was, however, eafy to fee he did not think fo; for, incapable of following advice he was fo folicitous to give, he could not forbear liftening at the door, going half-way up the ftairs, and fhewing many fymptoms of extreme inquietude. He dreaded, indeed, even the reftoration of Rofalie's fenfes, when he was affured fhe would immediately afk queftions; to which the folly of Claudine, or the matter of fact of the woman of the houfe, would give anfwers that might occafion the moft dangerous relapfe. Thefe uneafy apprehenfions were not appeafed by the appearance of the apothecary, who expreffed himfelf under the

greateft

greateſt alarm for the event, entreated that
the lady might be kept quiet, and that the
next viſit of the phyſician might be haſten-
ed.—Montalbert heard all this in a ſtate
of mind it is impoſſible to deſcribe. He
knew, indeed, that Roſalie was ill from
the report of Vyvian; but he knew not
how ill, having ſeen him only for a moment.

Now all her danger appeared to him
with redoubled terrors. From the little
explanation, which his paſſion would admit of during his ſhort and unfortunate
interview with Walſingham, he began to
doubt whether he had not been guilty at
once of ingratitude and cruelty, and whether he ſhould not now be puniſhed with
eternal remorſe, as well as by loſing Roſalie for ever. Still ardent and impetuous,
he inquired why he could not go or ſend
for the phyſician inſtantly—then not liſtening to any reaſons that were given him,
why it would be ineffectual, he ſtarted up,
demanded of Mr. Greenwood, the apothecary, his poſitive opinion as to the ſtate
of

of the lady above ftairs, and infifted upon being allowed himfelf to fee her. Againft this, however, Leffington remonftrated warmly, and Ormfby even angrily; while Mr. Greenwood protefted to him, that, if fhe was fubjected to any farther alarms, he would not anfwer for her life till morning. He faid that he had already been compelled to quiet her harraffed fpirits by a medicine for that purpofe; and if its effects were counteracted, fuch was the weaknefs of her frame, and fuch the nature of the fever which continually feized her, that the moft fatal effects would very probably follow: he then took his leave.

Montalbert threw himfelf into a chair, and gave himfelf up to the moft dreadful apprehenfions. Ormfby walked about the room in a ftate but little better, while Leffington, ever ufeful and compofed, afcended foftly to the chamber of the poor patient, whom he found fometimes uttering a few incoherent words in a low voice, then, with a deep figh, finking into filence. At length fhe feemed to become quite

tranquil;

tranquil; and Leffington having infifted on Claudine's leaving the room, and engaged the woman of the houfe, with one of her maids, to remain there, returned himfelf to Ormfby and Montalbert, whom he was not very willing to leave long together.

The inftant his immediate fears for Rofalie fubfided, the idea that Montalbert had deftroyed the unfortunate Walfingham recurred to the mind of Leffington. He fhuddered, and, at once pitying and condemning him, recollected that his perfon was not fafe; and if the event of his meeting with Walfingham had been as fatal as he reprefented it, he ought to haften from a country where he was liable to be feized as a murderer.

Montalbert fat immoveable; he feemed regardlefs of any danger that might threaten himfelf, but liftened to every noife in the houfe; and if he fancied any one ftirred in Rofalie's chamber, he ftarted, and eagerly afked Leffington if he thought fhe was awake and fenfible?

Ormfby,

Ormſby, overcome with fatigue and anxiety, had now been perſuaded to retire, and Leſſington remained alone with Montalbert.

It appeared to the former to be abſolutely neceſſary that Montalbert ſhould be reminded of his danger, or at leaſt that its extent might be known; taking occaſion then when he made ſome ſudden inquiry about his wife, Leſſington ſaid, " Allow me to remark to you, Mr. Montalbert, that your real tendernefs for our poor unfortunate Roſalie, of whoſe innocence I am ſure you will one day be perfectly convinced, cannot be ſo well ſhewn as by your recovering your preſence of mind in the preſent ſad conjuncture; and if the fatal event has happened, which you ſpoke of when you firſt arrived, you ſurely ought to think of your own ſafety, on which, I am ſure, the life of Roſalie muſt depend."

" Walſingham was not dead when I left him, (anſwered he mournfully); but I fear his wounds are mortal ! "

N 5   " Good

" Good God ! (exclaimed Leffington) ; and you remain here regardlefs of the event ? "

" Quite fo, (replied he), as far as re-lates to myfelf.—What have I left, that fhould make me wifh to preferve my life ? "

" Pray, (interrupted Leffington, who feared from his manner that he might re-lapfe into violence)—pray relate to me what has paffed fince you were feparated from my fifter ? "

Montalbert put his hand to his head, as if almoft unable to undertake the pain-ful tafk ; but Leffington, who had many reafons for wifhing to engage him in it, urging him again, he faid——

" I conclude you know the circumftances that fo ftrangely divided me from Rofa-lie.—I was returning to rejoin her in Si-cily ; having left my mother fo extremely difpleafed at my pofitive refufal to marry the lady fhe had chofen for me, that I in-tended merely to confult my wife before I declared our marriage, determining

to

to return to England, and to live in the humble and obfcure way our fortune demanded, till I became poffeffed of the property, however fmall, that muft be mine after my mother's deceafe.

" There were reafons that rendered our refidence in Sicily unpleafant to me, even when we were together; the frequent abfences, which our fear of my mother's difpleafure had obliged me to fubmit to, became daily more infupportable, and I was forming fchemes of retired happinefs when I had thrown off this cruel reftraint, and dared to be poor and independent. Judge then, how horrible were my feelings, when, awaking from this dream of felicity, I found Meffina in ruins, and the country for many miles around it convulfed by an earthquake, which had, two days before we made the coaft, buried half its inhabitants.

" I cannot tell you what were my fenfations after I had with much difficulty landed, for I have never fince been able to define them; nor do I know from whence

fprang

fprang the refolution with which I explored the place where the villa of Alozzi
had ftood, of which no other veftige remained than fome pieces of black and half-
burnt ruins: yet I looked with tearlefs
eyes into the dark chafms in which it was
funk, though I thought they but too furely
contained all I had loved—my Rofalie
and her child!

" The firft evening that I arrived at this
melancholy fpot, where I had fo lately left
the lovely treafures of my heart in apparent
fafety, there was none near it—I was undifturbed in my gloomy contemplation,
and remained lingering about the place,
till my fervant, who had followed me at
a diftance according to my direction, came
to me at night fall, and led me to a cottage
not far off, inhabited by a woman and
her daughter, who had loft the reft of their
family. Of thefe my fervant made fome
inquiries, as they were tenants of Count
Alozzi. He heard that the Count was
feen after the firft great fhock, and had
hired a veffel to take himfelf and fome

of

of his dependants to Naples; but whether he efcaped the fecond, or whether he was drowned with many others on the fudden reflux of the fea, thefe women had no means of knowing.—Here then was a glimpfe, and but a glimpfe of hope, that my wife and child might exift; but, on farther inquiry the next evening, I thought even this faint hope vanifhed. I knew that when I left Sicily, Alozzi was gone to Agrigentum, and was to ftay there fome time longer than I propofed remaining at Naples. It was not now, however, a time to confider much the caufe of his unexpected return. All my thoughts were bent on trying to recover from the ruins of his villa the fad remains of my loft family; and with this dreary fort of fatisfaction I occupied my mind, repairing the next day to the place, where I found three or four ftout peafants already at work.

" I inquired of them by whom they were employed?—they anfwered, in no very mild manner, by themfelves, and for their own purpofes and profit. I faw that

they

they feared I was difpofed, if not autho-
rifed, to impede their defigns; but by the
moft infallible of all arguments, (for I
emptied my purfe), and foon fatisfied them
that they fhould not be interrupted in the
poffeffion of whatever valuable effects they
might recover, fince my fole purpofe was
to fearch for the mangled relics of a wife
and child. I offered them more money
if they would procure farther affiftance to
expedite this fearch, and, explaining to
them who I was, promifed farther reward
if they could procure me any certain intelligence of Count Alozzi. They agreed
that he had been feen after the firft violent
concuffion of the earth; but all believed,
or affected to believe, he perifhed in the
fecond.

"It was now nine days fince the fatal
cataftrophe, three of which I ftood by
the yawning cavern that had fwallowed
the villa of Alozzi. Little was difcovered
by the men who went down among the
ruins; they were, indeed, more intent on
their own purpofes than on mine. On
the

the evening of the third day I went down myfelf, and I thought that by the remains of wainfcoting, or furniture, I fhould be led to the ruins of that part of the houfe Rofalie had inhabited. Defperate, I tore away, at fome rifk to myfelf, the door cafes, broken or fcorched pieces of building, and at length found the room where Rofalie ufually fat. I could clearly diftinguifh that there were no remains of human bodies in it; two only had been found, and they were known to be fervants; but though another day's fearch fatisfied that no more perfons were buried in thefe ruins, yet even this circumftance afforded no proof, that thofe my fickening foul inquired after were living.

" With an anxious and hopelefs heart I left the peafants bufily employed in labour, which had already amply repaid them, and now fat out to wander over the country, afking queftions of the unhappy perfons who were yet fcattered about it, though their anfwers only irritated my mifery, or confirmed my defpair.

Moft

Moſt of them were too much occupied by the wants and woes of their own condition, to give much attention to me. After ſome days were thus vainly waſted, I croſſed over to the other ſide of the iſland, and went among ſuch relations and friends of Alozzi as had eſcaped any immediate ſhare of the misfortune by being at a diſtance from that part where its violence had fallen. Among them I learned that Alozzi had quitted Agrigentum four or five days before the earthquake, and had gone, as they believed, to Meſſina, where they had no doubt of his having periſhed, as they had never heard of him ſince. There was hardly one of thoſe families who had not ſome relation or friend to lament; and I only quitted one houſe of mourning to enter another.

To me, all appeared equally deſolate and wretched; the image of my loſt happineſs continually haunted me, and I returned more unhappy than ever to the place where once ſtood the villa of Alozzi.

" By

" By this time fome peafants who had been difperfed, had come back to that neighbourhood alfo; among them I met two or three Sbirri, who were, I thought, likely perfons to have feen Alozzi, if he had indeed efcaped, for they were daring and active, and were probably bufy where-ever pay or plunder were likely to be had from the rich that furvived the earthquake. I entered into converfation with them, and heard that they had paffed the night, after the firft violent fhock, at a houfe belong-ing to the Count, where they had feen him with a lady and her child, and a Neapo-litan fervant. That they knew the lady was an Heretic from the woman of the houfe, who, as well as thofe to whom fhe had given fhelter during the horrors of that night, had expreffed their fears of re-maining under the fame roof with a perfon of that defcription, and that fome of the women had actually left it, left fhe fhould draw Divine vengeance on the houfe.

This afcertained, beyond a doubt, that it was my wife who accompanied Alozzi,

I now

I now endeavoured to trace her farther, with an eagernefs which thofe only can imagine, who, amidft the darkeft defpair, are fuddenly dazzled with a ray of hope. I inquired of every body—I offered money for the flighteft information, and fometimes paid it for accounts which I knew to be falfe. At length a man was brought to me, who affured me that he had converfed with Zulietta, the Neapolitan girl, whom he exactly defcribed, and who had told him that her miftrefs and Count Alozzi were gone to Naples, and fhe was only by accident left behind. He named the time when, and place where, he had feen Zulietta: I bade him lead me thither, but learned that this young woman was gone to Catanca, with a perfon.who had promifed to find a paffage for her to her home. To Catanca I followed her; fhe had left it a few days before with a family, who had taken her into their fervice, and was gone to Italy, but whether to Naples or not I could not learn. To Naples, however, I refolved to go, in order to purfue

the

the clue, which I hoped would lead me to the recovery of all I held moft dear upon earth.

" I had, however, loft above five weeks in Sicily, and on the voyage, which proved unufually tedious. At length I reached Naples, and, concealing myfelf with every poffible precaution from all who were likely to know me, I haftened to the houfe of Alozzi.

" The porter knew and admitted me. He told me that the Count had efcaped from Sicily, and had even remained a month afterwards at Naples, which he had left but a few days fince at a moment's notice, and without faying whither he was gone, or when he fhould return. As this was not unufual with him, there appeared nothing extraordinary in it to the fervant, who, when I queftioned him as to any lady who had with her a child, and who accompanied his mafter, he affured me he knew of none, with fuch an air of fimplicity, that I could not but believe he at leaft knew nothing of the arrival of

my

my wife with his mafter. A thoufand
fears, and of various forts, now affailed
me. I trembled at once for my Rofalie's
fafety, and even for her fidelity, if fhe
lived. . . . . . . All the fymptoms which I
thought I had formerly remarked of Alozzi's admiration, if not attachment, recurred
to me : he had not brought her to his own
houfe publicly as the wife of his friend,
whom he had affifted to efcape from de-
ftruction. This indeed might be accounted for by my fituation in regard to my
mother; but why was fhe fo carefully concealed from old and confidential fervants ?
I clofely queftioned them all, and could
not difcover that one of them had the leaft
knowledge of the Count's having refcued
my wife and child. They all declared
themfelves equally ignorant whither he was
gone; he had taken only his valet with
him. On farther minute inquiry, however, I difcovered that, for two or three
days before his departure, he had appeared
very uneafy and reftlefs; was frequently
fhut up with his own man for a confiderable

ble time after he had been running about
on bufinefs, which, though it was a profound fecret, feemed by his manner to be
of great importance. I paffed a whole
day in thefe examinations, and, in attempting to trace the road Alozzi had
taken, determined to follow and overtake
him. I found that he was gone towards
Florence, and thither I impatiently haftened.

" I arrived at the houfe, whither I with
difficulty had followed his track, the very
moment he was ftepping into his carriage,
about which his baggage announced his
being on a journey; when I advanced and
fpoke to him—he changed colour, hefitated, and trembled; I begged of him to go
back with me for a moment, and, without
farther preface, afked him what was become of my wife?

' What is become of her, Montalbert!
(faid he, ftill more agitated);—Do *you*
know nothing of her?'

' I know

' I know (faid I) that fhe left Sicily with you—that you have fince concealed her fomewhere.'

' I hope (added he, in a hafty and faltering voice) that you alfo know, then, for which of your Englifh friends fhe chofe to quit fuch protection as I was able to offer her, and in which fhe might undoubtedly have remained fafe till your return.' - - - - - - -

' My Englifh friends! (cried I)—what Englifh friends?—How could fhe meet them?—and - - - - - - -'

" But I fhould never conclude what I have to relate to you, Mr. Leffington, were I to repeat the long difcourfe that paffed. Alozzi told me a very plaufible ftory of his fudden return to Meffina; of his having fought and faved Rofalie and her child; and of his having afterwards placed her in a retired lodging, where, after a ftay of near a month, during which he had done every thing in his power to

tranquillize

tranquillize and footh her with the hopes
of my return, fhe became extremely difcontented; infifted on his trying to intereft for her fome Englifhman at Naples,
with whom fhe might return to her own
country; ' and, on my refufing to do fo,
(faid Alozzi), fhe attempted, as I found
afterwards, to bribe the fervants I had
placed about her, to deliver letters for
her to any Englifh gentlemen they could
hear of. Thefe people have protefted to
me, that they refifted every attempt fhe
made to engage them in this refearch :—
nor could I ever difcover by what means
Mrs. Montalbert contrived to find the
perfon with whom fhe concerted her meafures fo well, as to efcape during the
night, and to leave no trace by which I
have fince been able to difcover whither
fhe is gone; though I have hardly flept
fince, my dear friend, fo anxious have I
been to recover, if poffible, this lovely
mifguided wanderer, and to reftore her
to you, as a precious depofit of which I
was not an unworthy guardian!'

" I then

" I then inquired of Alozzi, if he had come to Florence on any hope of finding her there. He told me he had, but that all his inquiries being baffled, he was departing for Rome, ftill on the fame fearch. This was not enough for me; I infifted on his particularizing the reafons he had to believe my wife had gone to Florence; this he appeared ready to do, and I thought them fo plaufible, that I refolved to go among my countrymen, who were then numerous at Florence, in hopes of learning fomething of my poor fugitive. This inquiry, which detained me a great while, and which it was extremely painful to make on fo delicate a fubject, ended only in convincing me that fhe was not at Florence; and though, from repeated converfations with Alozzi, I was far from being fatisfied that Rofalie had not very different reafons for withdrawing herfelf from his protection, than thofe he had given, yet her impatience to be in England, or among perfons of her own country, if not a partiality to fome individual

of

of it, made me only waver between doubt and defpair, and happinefs feemed certainly fled for ever.''

Montalbert appeared fo exhaufted, that Leffington intreated him to take fome refrefhment; after which, all remaining quiet in the houfe, he thus continued his narrative.

CHAP. XXXVIII.

"WHITHER was I now to go in search of Rosalie? mistrusting as I did Alozzi, and doubting when he affected to be most busy in the pursuit, whether he had not himself concealed her. I determined, however, not to part with him— if his intentions were honest, he might assist me in my search; if not, I should at least have the chance of detecting him, by his endeavours to evade me, or by some of those oversights by which the most artful men often betray themselves.

" I therefore accompanied Alozzi to Rome, where we made acquaintance with every Englishman, and endeavoured to discover from them the names of their countrymen who had within a few weeks left Rome for England, or any part of Italy;

Italy; and in fhort made fuch enquiries as might lead to the objeft of our painful re-fearch. We gained, however, no fatis-faftion till at the end of a fortnight, when Alozzi came to tell me, he had met a *valet de place*, who had been accuftomed to live much with the Englifh at Rome; Alozzi faid, the man was remarkably in-telligent; that he had entered into dif-courfe with him, and found that about three weeks before he had ferved (though for a few days only) an Englifhman of the name of Walfingham, who came from Naples, attended by a young lady with whom this man believed he had 'eloped; for that his conduft while at Rome feemed calculated to baffle purfuit and enquiry, and that after a fhort time they departed very myfterioufly, but he had good reafons to believe they went to Genoa, there to embark for England. Alozzi brought the man to me; I queflioned him, and from his defcription I foon thought that Rofalie was the lady whom he had feen with Mr. Walfingham. I heard with anguifh not

to

to be expreffed that fhe was gay in fpirits, and accompanied this Walfingham evidently by her own confent. She had no child with her; but if fhe had fo far forgotten the father, as to follow another, fhe would have found no difficulty in abandoning her child.—The longer I talked with this man, the more clearly the fatal conviction flafhed upon me.—The time anfwered exactly to that on which Rofalie left the houfe where Alozzi had placed her: the character of Walfingham was that of a man of boundlefs expence, and unreftrained libertinifm; all ferved to perfuade my fenfes that he had ftolen from me the perfon and the affections of Rofalie.—Indignation and rage now animated a purfuit, which had before been prompted by tendernefs and hope. With whatever refentment I thought of the infidelity of my wife, my heart turned with fondnefs towards my child, thus abandoned, as I imagined, to the mercy of ftrangers, yet I knew not where to feek him; and the defire of vengeance was even ftronger than

than parental affection. After some con
sultation with Alozzi, it was agreed tha
he should return to Naples, where, by of
fering rewards, he had no doubt but h
should discover my son, of whom he pro
tested he would take a father's care, an
send him to me by some trusty person
whithersoever I should direct. Alozz
departed, and I made the best of my way
to Genoa; thither I traced persons resem
bling those I pursued, and on searching
the registers kept at the *Dogana*, of peopl
departing from that port, I found tha
about a fortnight before my arrival, Mr
Walsingham, an Englishman, with hi
lady and two servants, had embarked fo
England.

" I had now no doubts remaining—Ro
salie passed for the wife of Walsingham
and as such was proceeding to her nativ
country.

" Stung even to temporary madness, I
adopted the sudden resolution of writing
to my mother, reproaching her with the
misery she had been the cause of, by com
pellin

pelling me to take meafures which had torn from me the woman I adored, and with her all the happinefs of my life; I told her that to make me any amends was impoffible; that I fhould never fee her more; but that if fhe were not totally loft to every feeling of humanity, I implored her to receive and protect my child, whom, by a letter written at the fame time to Alozzi, I defired him to fend to her. I hoped that even her bitter and inveterate prejudices might give way to pity and concern, when *I* could no longer offend her, and when fhe faw in a lovely and innocent infant the reprefentative of a fon whom fhe had driven to defpair.

" Having done this, I gave myfelf up wholly to that thirft of vengeance which devoured me, and took my paffage to England in the firft fhip I could meet with, but for which I had the mortification of waiting a confiderable time.

" Every perverfe accident, to which a traveller by fea is fubject, confpired to retard my paffage. The fhip was old, and

a had

a bad failer; the captain had not enough
men to work it, and of the few he had,
two were confined to their hammocks by
an infectious fever. We were continually
beaten back by contrary winds, and the
mortality increafed in our little crew fo
much, that when we came into the Strait,
I infifted upon being put on fhore at
Gibraltar, where, having taken the fever,
I became extremely ill, and, after a confinement of near a month, narrowly efcaped
with my life. This cruel delay over, I
once more embarked in a floop of war,
and was at length landed at Plymouth.
In London I could not fail to hear of Mr.
Walfingham, for there a man of his fortune muft be known. I obtained a direction to his houfe in Grofvenor Street,
where I heard that he was juft gone to
Brighthelmftone. I could no longer entertain a fingle doubt of my being right
as to the perfon, for on enquiry of his
fervants I heard, that he was, a few weeks
fince, returned from a tour to Italy.

o 4   " I haf-

" I haftened, therefore, to Brighthelmftone, and to a houfe taken for the feafon
by this Mr. Walfingham; I heard he was
gone on a failing party to Portfmouth and
the Ifle of Wight, but was expected back
in a few days: his character anfwered to
all I had heard of him abroad. Afraid of
miffing if I attempted to follow him, I refolved to await his return; but fleep forfook my pillow, and I wandered about
from the dawn of the day, till the lateft
hour of night, without any other purpofe
than to wear away the tedious time that
prevented my doing myfelf juftice. It
happened that I was fitting at a very early
hour of the morning in one of the public
libraries, where two of thofe *bon vivans*
were alfo fitting, who regularly make
tours during the fummer months round
the coaft, to repair the exceffes of their
winter. I fat penfively filent, thinking on
fubjects, how different; when thefe two
good cits began a difcourfe on the various
advantages or difadvantages of different
bathing places: one related to the other,
that

that he had lately left Eaftbourne; where, faid he, ' I got poultry pretty reafonable, and the wheat-ears were beginning to flock. There was not, indeed, much company; but then there were people that cared not what they gave for any thing; there was the famous Lady Llancarrick, and a Mifs Something, one of your book-making ladies, with her. To be fure I thought it a little oddifh to fee her Lady-fhip quite hand and glove not only with that Mifs What-d'ye-call'um, but with another young creature, who goes, you muft know, by the name of Sheffield, but as the people there fay, is the miftrefs of one Mr. Wal-fingham, a man of great fortune, who brought her from abroad.—My fon Jack, who came down to me from Friday to Tuefday, and is a mighty chap for a pretty face, fell downright in love with this fine madam—though, to do her juftice, fhe looks very modeft for one of that fort; and egad, Sir, it was as much as I could do to keep him from making up to her—Why,

Jack,

Jack, (fays I), don't you fee fhe is coun-
tenanced by Lady Llancarrick. He
laughed, and faid, the lady herfelf was no
better than fhe fhould be, and he'd make
love to them all three.'

" Imagine, Mr. Leffington, what I felt
at hearing this converfation.—I knew not
what I faid to the man, but he told me,
with many bows, and fome gafping gri-
maces, all he knew; among other particulars, that the lady had a child with her;
and then they both walked away, probably
much amazed at my inquifitivenefs and
violence; while liftening to nothing but
my rage and indignation, I ordered a poft-
chaife, and taking a lawyer with me, and
a perfon to attend on the child, I fat out
for Eaftbourne: as you have heard Rofalie's account, you know that I faw her
but for a moment: I could not indeed
bear to look upon her—fhe was walking
with the two women I had heard defcribed:—I fled from her, and directing
my fon to be brought to me, I haftened
back in a ftate of diftraction, weeping

over the innocent unhappy boy, now accufing his mother of cruelty, and now
protefting I would never think of her
more.

" I believe nothing faved me from attempting my own life, but my determined
refolution to obtain fatisfaction of Walfingham.—I waited a few days longer, and
when he was returned, I fent to him a
military friend, whom I met by accident,
and who told me he was flightly acquainted with Walfingham. I ftated my com-
plaint, and this friend, Captain Wilmot,
carried him a challenge from me, to meet
at any hour he appointed the next day.

" When Wilmot came back, he affured
me, that Walfingham was extremely willing to meet me, if I infifted on it; but
that he protefted he knew not for what,
having never feen Mrs. Montalbert in his
life, and being totally unconfcious of having ever done me the leaft injury. This
falfehood only irritated my impatience—
But Wilmot advifed me to recollect whether there might not be fome miftake in

all

all this? ' I do not,' faid he, ' know much
of Sommers Walfingham, but I am fure
his courage is not to be doubted; and as
to an affair of gallantry, he is much more
likely to boaft of, than to deny it. I am
perfuaded, that had he eloped with Mrs.
Montalbert, he would very readily have
given you the fatisfaction you demand.'—
More enraged than ever at what I could
not but think a bafe and cowardly evafion,
and almoft ready to quarrel with Wilmot
himfelf, I was determined to feek Walfingham inftantly, and compel him to give
an explanation—but Wilmot, who faw that
fome mifchief muft happen if I did, prevailed upon me to let him return once
more to Walfingham.—He came back in
about an hour, and declared to me that
Walfingham had given him fuch a detail
of the circumftances of his life for the laft
fix months, that he was perfectly convinced he had never had the flighteft acquaintance with Mrs. Montalbert.—'Good
God!' exclaimed I; ' this is *too* much—
did I not trace him from Rome to Genoa;

do

do I not know that the woman who accompanied him muſt have been my wife?'

'My dear friend,' ſaid Wilmot, 'Walſingham acknowledges that he had a lady with him, but declares it was not Mrs. Montalbert.—He has told me who it was, and, if you inſiſt upon it, the lady who is not far from hence will ſatisfy you as to her identity. Can you ſuppoſe, Montalbert (added Wilmot, very gravely), that I have ſo little regard for you, or hold your honour of ſo little moment, that I would trifle with, or deceive you? If you inſiſt on fighting, I am ready to attend you.—But I repeat, that in the grounds of this quarrel I do believe you are wrong.'— I knew Wilmot to be a man of unblemiſhed honour, and of undoubted courage; and though it yet ſeemed impoſſible that I could be deceived, I heſitated. At that moment Charles Vyvian came to me.

'Not leſs raſh, or leſs irritated than myſelf, for he had read Sommers Walſingham's letter, Wilmot (who was even more acquainted with him than with me), had

had

had the greateſt difficulty imaginable to perſuade him to hear what he had to ſay. At length it was ſettled, that as he knew the perſon of my wife, he ſhould go with Wilmot to the lady; and if he was convinced that ſhe had accompanied Walſingham from Italy, which he thought he ſhould eaſily diſcover, it was agreed that I could have no quarrel with him.—This lady was at a ſmall town, about twenty miles from Brighthelmſtone, on the London road; and thither my friends repaired, with the conſent of Sommers Walſingham. Towards evening I expeɛted their return; I went out alone upon the hills, where I was accóſted by a gentleman, whom my ſervant had, at his own requeſt, accompanied in ſearch of me. He told me, with very little preface, that his name was Walſingham; that on hearing I was in ſearch of him, and that ſome diſagreeable circumſtances were likely to happen by my having miſtaken for him a relation of the ſame name, he had come from Eaſtbourne on purpoſe to give me the explanation I demanded.

demanded. I will not repeat to you the manner in which I treated Mr. Walsingham; my trembling fervant, who dared not difobey me, brought the loaded piftols I fent him for; I abfolutely refufed to hear what Walfingham would have faid.—The words, ' I came from Eaftbourne;' and ' *it* WAS *I—who accompanied Mrs. Montalbert from Italy*,' were enough for me.— When he found me deaf to his intended vindication, he took a piftol, and bade me fire mine.—I did fo—with too good an aim! the ball lodged in his fide; he did not however fall: but firing his piftol in the air, he beckoned to my fervant, whom I had driven with menaces to fome diftance; the poor fellow ran to him, and Walfingham, who had thrown away his piftol, leaning againft him, faid, ' I am wounded—I believe mortally: lay me on the ground; go call fome perfons to be witneffes that your mafter has acted like a man of honour, and that I acquit him of my death.'—I had in the mean time approached him; and guilty as I ftill believed

him,

him, I could not fee the palenefs of death on his face without anguifh and remorfe; he was lying on the ground, and feemed, amidft the pain which his countenance ex-preffed, more folicitous for my fafety than for his own life.—Touched by his generofity, I bade my man fly for fur-geons: and when he was gone, I knelt by the fuffering Walfingham with fenfations of mingled rage and regret, which cannot be defcribed, while he thus fpoke to me:

'Mr. Montalbert, it is probable I have but a few hours to live:—hear me, I con-jure you, when I declare upon the honour of a dying man, that your wife is as inno-cent as an angel; that I have ever treated her as a beloved fifter; and that you will be guilty of the moft cruel injuftice in throwing her from you. I have not breath to tell you by what ftrange circumftance it happened that I was the inftrument to releafe her from the power of your mo-ther, who had confined her at Formifcufa. I feel very faint.—They tell me you have taken your child from her, and that fhe

is

is reduced to the brink of the grave by forrow..... Reftore her child—reftore to her your affections, and try to make her happy—fhe deferves all your tendernefs; and—if it fhould happen, as I am per-fuaded it will, that you are convinced you have been too rafh—let not any remorfe for what has happened difturb your tran-quillity.—*I* am a being, who have long been weary of life—and for me Death has no horrors.—*You* may for many years con-ftitute and fhare the happinefs of an ami-able woman; and it is fome fatisfaction to me, to think you will one day know that I was incapable of injuring you.'

" He fpoke flowly and with difficulty—*I* was incapable of anfwering!—but again he earneftly urged me to fave myfelf by flight.—I incoherently told him, I hoped his wound was not mortal.—' I hope not, (faid he)—but if it fhould, I intreat you, for the fake of Mrs. Montalbert, to take care of yourfelf.'—By this time my fer-vant was come up with a furgeon; before he could decide whether the wound was

likely

likely to be fatal, or how he could attempt moving poor Walfingham, Sommers Walfingham, Wilmot, and Vyvian, arrived together with a chair, which they had the precaution to bring with them.

" I cannot relate what now paffed.—Before the wounded man would confent to be moved, he infifted that the perfons prefent fhould liften to the folemn declaration he made, that I had ufed him honourably, and was in no way to blame. I own this magnanimity, from a man whom I have perhaps injured, has deeply affected me. He bade my friends infift on my leaving the place, and Vyvian, I hardly knew how, forced me into a poft chaife as foon as he had feen Walfingham's wound probed ; for, till he had brought me fome intelligence of him, I would not ftir.— The furgeon had not yet attempted to extract the ball ; nor could they pronounce with any certainty, but they entertained great fears for his life. Sommers Walfingham went off to London exprefs, to bring down fome very eminent man of

the

the profeffion; and at the repeated in-
treaties of Walfingham I came hither, without, however, meaning to withdraw myfelf
from any inquiry that may be made—
if he dies ! ------

' You will, I fear, have too much reafon to reproach yourfelf, (interrupted Leffington).——You never received then a
letter, which, from her journal, I fee our
poor Rofalie fent to you from Marfeilles,
under cover to the Englifh Ambaffador at
Naples ? '

' Never! (replied Montalbert).—But
has my wife then kept a journal—and may
I not fee it ? '

' If you will be calm, (faid Leffington),
I will put it into your hands.'——Montalbert, fubdued as he was, and beginning
to be confcious of his own rafhnefs, promifed all that was afked of him; and in
this perufal paffed the reft of the night;
Leffington continually going to the door
of Rofalie's chamber, where he found her
much more quiet than he had ventured to
expect.

At

At a very early hour of the morning, two poſt chaiſes ſtopped near the houſe. From one of them came Vyvian, with the little Montalbert and his maid; from the other, the phyſician who had attended Roſalie......Poor Montalbert ſaw them enter without having the power to ſpeak. He queſtioned by looks the countenance of Vyvian, but found nothing that encouraged him to aſk after Walſingham.—Vyvian, however, underſtood him, and ſaid, " Walſingham is alive, and his caſe not deſperate, though certainly dangerous."

" Thank God! (exclaimed Montalbert), I may yet then taſte of ſatisfaction !"—— " Be not too ſanguine, (anſwered Vyvian); but I am all impatience to know the ſtate of our poor Roſalie !"——Overcome by ſenſations ſo acute and various, Montalbert ſat in breathleſs anxiety; his tears fell on the face of his child as he preſſed him to his heart, and he caſt an earneſt look towards the door, as he heard the ſteps of the phyſician deſcending from Roſalie's room.

He

He gave, however, a better account of her than they had dared to promise themselves; and, as he had heard from Vyvian a sketch of her story in consequence of his attendance on Walfingham, he ventured to advise that Rosalie might, as soon as possible, have her child restored to her, and be told that her husband was returned.

" Mrs. Montalbert's illness, (said he), is so evidently occasioned by uneasiness and fear, that my art can do nothing while those causes exist; remove them, and she will soon, I believe, be restored to health."

Montalbert then ventured to say—" But, Sir, if this unfortunate Mr. Walfingham should die?"

" I hope, though I cannot say he will not!" answered Dr. F———.

" But at all events, (interrupted Ormsby, who having heard what had passed, now joined them)—at all events let my daughter see her little boy; and you, Sir, (continued he, turning to Montalbert)—you, I hope, will now do her justice—you will."

" It

" It is not yet time, dear Mr. Ormſby, (ſaid Leſſington), to diſcuſs many points, which, I hope, we ſhall amicably talk over hereafter... .Mr. Montalbert allows that the conduct of my ſiſter has been unexceptionable, and that of Mr. Walſingham moſt generous."

" It is I only, (ſaid Montalbert, in a mournful and ſomewhat ſtern voice)—it is I alone who have been to blame."

Leſſington, fearful of what might follow, cried haſtily—" We can none of us think that.—Alas! which of us, ſituated as you were, might not have acted as you did!"

Dr. F——— now departed, promiſing to ſend a meſſenger from Brighthelmſtone, with the opinion of the ſurgeons, as ſoon as the gentleman (Sommers Walſingham) expected was arrived; and Leſſington went up to prepare Roſalie for the ſight of her child.

She had no ſooner in her arms this darling of her affections, than ſhe ſeemed to have obtained a new exiſtence. Leſſington

ton thought he might then venture to tell her, at leaſt a part, of what had paſſed, concealing, however, the ſad effects of Montalbert's paſſionate ſuſpicions.

When he told her, her huſband was in the houſe, ſhe declared herſelf able to ſee him—for the ſlight view ſhe had of him before ſeemed like a dream. She no ſooner beheld him, than ſhe attempted, but vainly attempted, to ſpeak, while he, far from yielding to thoſe tranſports of joy which he would have felt had not Walſingham been in danger, was wretched, though apparently reſtored to the boſom of happineſs; and ſhuddered, as he thought, that Roſalie was perhaps embracing the murderer of her generous preſerver, and one who might ſoon be an exile from her and from his country!

This painful ſuſpenſe continued ſome days, for the ſituation of Walſingham was long doubtful after the arrival of his ſurgeon from London. Roſalie, though ſhe did not yet leave her room, for ſhe continued extremely weak, could not fail to

remark

remark the gloom that hung over her friends, and particularly Montalbert, who often fell into deep and melancholy reveries; then, fuddenly ftarting, liftened to any noife in the houfe, watched every one entering at the door, and feemed frequently fo uneafy, that Rofalie, however, willing to impute his inquietude to the fituation he was in with regard to his mother, which he had told her of, could not but difcover that fomething of more immediate import preffed on his mind; fhe had never ventured fince their reconciliation to name Walfingham.—Too well aware from the flight and half-ftifled narrative fhe had received from her brother and her father, that Montalbert's jealoufy had been the caufe of the ftep he had taken as to her child, fhe feared to awaken it anew by naming him, while Montalbert, obferving her caution, felt hurt that fhe did not fpeak of him openly and candidly—and thefe concealed fenfations on both fides occafioned a fort of reftraint that rendered them far from happy.

As

As Rofalie every day became better, and thought herfelf well enough to leave a place which reminded her of many days of fufpenfe and uneafinefs, fhe felt fome furprife that neither her father nor Montalbert propofed her removal, for they had concealed from her their debates on this fubject, which had not paffed without fome afperity on Montalbert's part. Confcious of high birth, and of his right to an ample property, he did not reflect, without bitternefs of heart, on his reverfe of fortune.—Inftead of raifing his wife to high affluence, he found himfelf and his fon now almoft entirely dependent on Mr. Ormfby, who, though related to him by blood, the notions he had acquired among foreign nobility taught him to confider as a merchant and an adventurer for gain. Ormfby, on the other hand, had been fo long ufed to the moft perfect obedience to his will from every body about him, that he was hurt at the little fubmiffion which Montalbert fhewed to his wifhes, when he expreffed an intention of making a confi-

derable

derable purchafe, and placing Rofalie a miftrefs of his houfe and fortune. Montalbert fancied that Ormfby would not be forry if the fatal termination of Walfing-ham's accident compelled him to go a-broad; but fecretly determined, if it did that no confiderations of intereft fhould in-duce him to leave his wife and child in England.—Ormfby was not only confcious that he fhould have been happier to have found his daughter fingle, but fancied the fentiment juftified by the pride and vio-lence which he thought natural to Mon-talbert's chara&er.

These heart-burnings between two per-fons, on whom the happinefs of Rofalie fo entirely depended, gave extreme con-cern to Leffington, and kept him from returning home, notwithftanding the re-peated letters he received from his wife. Vyvian faw with equal concern that there was no cordiality between them; but the fituation of Walfingham, whom he had twice vifited, and whofe chara&er had im-

preffed

preffed him with the higheft efteem, was a fource of ftill deeper regret.

How ftrange is the difpofition of human events! Rofalie, who but a very few days back fuffered every poffible calamity, now faw her hufband returned, her child re-ftored, her father in fafety, and mafter of an ample fortune (circumftances which even in her moft fanguine moments fhe never ventured to flatter herfelf with); yet, with all thefe bleffings united, Rofalie was not happy; and had fhe known the fituation of Walfingham, would have been extremely miferable.

Convinced, however, that fomething very ferious occafioned the reftleffnefs and anxiety which feemed to increafe on every face that approached her, from fome un-guarded expreffions, as well as from the extreme folicitude with which they had been explained away, Rofalie caught fome vague fufpicions of the truth, fhe con-trived to queftion Claudine fo narrowly, that the poor girl, who had long been

fadly

sadly overweighed with the secret, burst into tears, and disclosed all she knew.

Disqualified as Rosalie was to bear such a shock, the necessity of supporting it with calmness immediately occurred to her. Claudine, already terrified at what she had done, besought her to say nothing to Mr. Ormsby, whom she heard upon the stairs— but her countenance betrayed too evidently what passed: hardly, however, had she time to attempt evading her father's questions, when Montalbert appeared, and the necessity of her artificial tranquillity became more pressing. Vyvian and Lessington were walking; something like conversation was attempted between Ormsby and Montalbert, but it would have flagged, if Claudine, who dreaded their observations, had not opportunely brought the child, in whom they all took an equal interest. A packet, however, was brought into the room by the mistake of a servant, on which Montalbert had no sooner cast his eyes, than he changed countenance, and betrayed such violent emotion, that Rosalie,

Rofalie, concluding Walfingham was dead, had only refolution enough left to avoid betraying, otherwife than by her features, the extreme pain this idea gave her. Montalbert, trembling with impatient dread, tore the letter half open : then recollecting himfelf, haftened out of the room, and Ormfby, who guessed that it brought fome fatal intelligence, followed him.

The letter, however, inftead of bringing to Montalbert the cruel intelligence he expected, was to this effect :

" DEAR SIR,
" I have infifted on being allowed to write this letter, to fatisfy thofe fears which the people about me have, I know, given you. My friend Bernard permits me to tell you myfelf, that he believes I fhall in a few days be well enough to remove by flow journies to London, whither his bufinefs calls him fo preffingly, that he can no longer attend me here; and as we have been friends from our childhood, I find myfelf fo much happier in his than in other

P 3   hands,

hands, whatever may be their ſkill, that I am reſolved to accompany him. You will conclude from this, that all the dangerous ſymptoms which have hung about me are removed; and I truſt that the pain this affair has given you will no longer interrupt your preſent happineſs.——For you muſt be happy, Montalbert, with ſo amiable a woman!

" As ſoon as I am quite well I ſhall return to the Continent.——Conſider whether I can do you any ſervice with Signora Belcaſtro. Is it not poſſible, that, from miſrepreſentations, her general prejudice may have been raiſed into particular diſlike?——I own to you, that from Mrs. Montalbert's account, as well as from other circumſtances, I fear Alozzi has been leſs ſincerely your friend than you have believed. Perhaps I may be the fortunate means of undeceiving your mother; and you will really oblige me, by giving me an opportunity of being uſeful to you, either in this or in any other way.

" If

" If Vyvian would come over to fee
me, before I go, it would give me pleafure.—I hope our friendfhip, however un-
pleafantly begun, will be permanent.—
Permit me to offer to Mrs. Montalbert
my moft refpeftful good wifhes; my dear
little ward and fellow-traveller, is not old
enough to remember me, but I fhall always
recolleft him with pleafure. Adieu, dear
Sir, I have exceeded Bernard's permiffion,
and muft haftily affure you, that I am
your moft faithful fervant,

" F. WALSINGHAM."

This letter, though evidently written
in pain and languor, took from the heart
of Montalbert fuch a weight, that he feemed fuddenly reftored to happinefs and reafon. He determined to go over himfelf
with Vyvian to vifit this generous man,
who had fuffered fo much for his ineftima-
ble fervices, and unparalleled goodnefs,
and, forgetting all his former precautions,
he was haftening to fhew the letter to Rofalie, as foon as her father had read it,

when

when the entrance of Leffington and Vyvian prevented him.

Montalbert and Vyvian agreed to fet out immediately, and Leffington undertook to relate to Rofalie the truths which had been fo long concealed from her.—He found her already informed of all but the late relief from their apprehenfions. She could not hear of the fufferings of her benefactor, and of his unexampled generofity, without great emotion : Leffington bade her indulge it, but ftill fearing left Montalbert fhould again feel fufpicions, which had already coft him fo much, fhe tried to check her tears when Montalbert appeared—but it was impoffible. And he, by a thoufand tender apologies, intreated her to forgive his rafhnefs and injuftice, and encouraged her to indulge thofe tears, which a little relieved her oppreffed heart.

Montalbert, Leffington, and Vyvian, now fet out on their vifit; the two latter took leave of Rofalie : Leffington returning

into

into Oxfordshire, and Vyvian having determined to accompany Walsingham to London.

During the short absence of her husband, Ormsby talked over with his daughter their future plans of life. It was probable that Montalbert, however his pride might be hurt, would not now oppose the wishes of Ormsby, who seemed to place all his satisfaction in bestowing on his daughter a degree of affluence, which should set her even above the daughters of Vyvian, who had despised and contemned her: but Rosalie represented to her father, that, beyond a certain point, fortune contributed nothing to real happiness; that whatever attracted towards her the eyes of the world, would quicken the envy and malignity with which her story would be related, and could not fail to reflect on the beloved memory of her mother. To this argument Ormsby was compelled to yield, and he found himself under the necessity, however painful, of continuing to conceal from the world the relationship in which

he

he ftood to Rofalie, wifhing it to remain as much a fecret as a circumftance
could do already known to fo many perfons, and which, during Rofalie's illnefs,
no pains had been taken to conceal.

Montalbert returned more deeply impreffed than ever with the generofity of
Walfingham. He had, however, paid all
the pecuniary obligations Rofalie owed
him, and they parted with mutual profeffions of friendfhip.

In a few days afterwards Mr. and Mrs.
Montalbert, and their little boy, went
round the coaft into Kent, and took a
houfe near Margate for the reft of the
fummer, while Ormfby made a tour through
the weftern counties in fearch of a purchafe for his daughter, where, at a fmall
diftance, he might find a refidence for
himfelf.

Montalbert, whofe natural infirmities of
temper had been chaftifed and correated
by the events which had fo nearly deprived
him of the felicity he enjoyed, feemed now
to think that he could never make fufficient
amends

amends to his charming wife for the injury he had done her, by giving way to fufpicions fhe fo little deferved. About three months after his removal to London, Walfingham went to Italy, where, by means of fome Italian friends of high rank, he procured an introduction to Signora Belcaftro, and gradually contrived to inform her of the fhare he had had in delivering her daughter-in-law from her ufurped power, while he undeceived her in regard to many reprefentations made by Alozzi, who, finding himfelf baffled in defigns, which the abfence and probable death of Montalbert had occafioned him to form, had really been, in his turn, the dupe of Signora Belcaftro, and had followed the fcent fhe had arfully given, that Rofalie had eloped with an Englifhman.——Walfingham acquired fo much influence over the mind of this ftrange woman, that though he could not prevail upon her to forgive her fon for having married as he did, fhe at length relented in favour of his children, and

fettled

settled upon them what she had intended for their father, to whom, however, her pride and Walsingham's persuasions prevailed upon her to allow a handsome annual income.

Montalbert enjoyed, at a small but beautiful place on the coast of Dorsetshire, with which Ormsby had presented his wife, more happiness than usually falls to the lot of humanity. Rosalie passed her life in studying how to contribute to his felicity, and that of her father, and, by her sweetness and attention, she won them both from those little asperities and difference of temper which had once threatened to destroy their domestic comfort.

But notwithstanding the cheerful and even gay letters which Walsingham wrote to his friends, letters which greatly contributed to the happiness of Rosalie, who retained for him the most grateful regard, he was still an unhappy wanderer; and when he had done all he could to restore Montalbert to his mother's favour, and

was

was no longer animated by the hope of
ferving Rofalie, he funk again into that
cold defpondence, which a fenfible heart
feels when the world around is as a defart.
The agonies with which he had wept over
the grave of his Leonora had been fufpended by the almoft imperceptible attachment which had crept into his bofom
for Rofalie, and which he had indulged
but too much, after there appeared fome
probability that Montalbert was no more.

The laft letters he wrote to England
informed his friends that he was fetting
out on a tour through Spain and Portugal; and that finding himfelf more than
ever difpofed to wander, he thought it
not improbable but that he might go from
thence to the Cape, and fo to the Eaft
Indies.——In the purfuit of fcience and
knowledge he found confolation, when no
benevolent action offered itfelf to fatisfy
his philanthrophy ; but fo generally is mifery diffufed, that there were few places
which did not offer objects for this indulgence—though none could intereft him
like

like the amiable Being whom he had re-leafed from the dreary confinement of Formifcufa, and reftored to the poffeffion of the happinefs fhe now enjoyed—a hap-pinefs which alone could foften the fad-nefs of his own deftiny!!!

THE END.